the innocent Polly McDoodle

For Jessica
all the best
Mary Woodbury

the innocent Polly McDoodle

Mary Woodbury

COTEAU BOOKS
TWENTY-FIVE YEARS

Edited by Barbara Sapergia.
Cover painting by Ward Schell.
Interior map illustration by Linda Hendry.
Cover and book design by Duncan Campbell.
Typeset by Karen Steadman.
Printed and bound in Canada by Veilleux Impression À Demande Inc.

Canadian Cataloguing in Publication Data

Mary Woodbury, 1935-
The innocent Polly McDoodle
ISBN 1-55050-168-2

1. Title.

PS8595.0644 I56 2000   jC813'.54   C00–920164–5
PZ7.W85955 In 2000

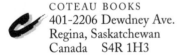

COTEAU BOOKS
401-2206 Dewdney Ave.
Regina, Saskatchewan
Canada   S4R 1H3

AVAILABLE IN THE US FROM
General Distrubution Services
4500 Witmer Industrial Estates
Niagara Falls, NY,   14305-1386

The publisher gratefully acknowledges the financial assistance of the
Saskatchewan Arts Board, the Canada Council for the Arts, the Government
of Canada through the Book Publishing Industry Development Program
(BPIDP), and the City of Regina Arts Commission, for its publishing program.

*This one is dedicated to Robert Woodbury
and his daughter Carys.*

contents

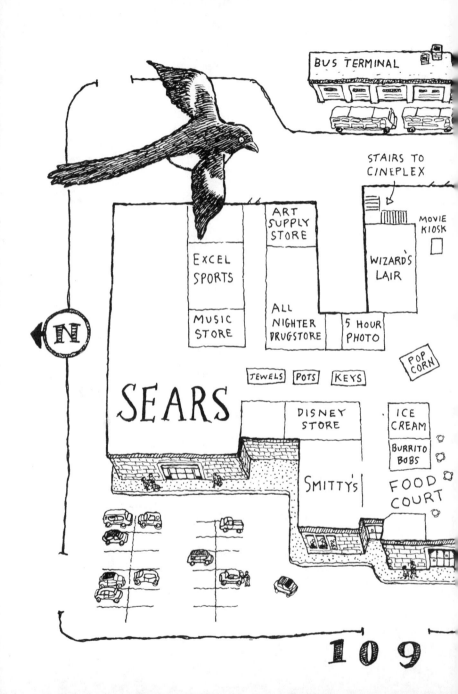

BUS TERMINAL

STAIRS TO CINEPLEX

MOVIE KIOSK

ART SUPPLY STORE

EXCEL SPORTS

MUSIC STORE

ALL NIGHTER DRUGSTORE

5 HOUR PHOTO

WIZARD'S LAIR

N

POP CORN

JEWELS POTS KEYS

SEARS

DISNEY STORE

ICE CREAM

BURRITO BOBS

SMITTY'S

FOOD COURT

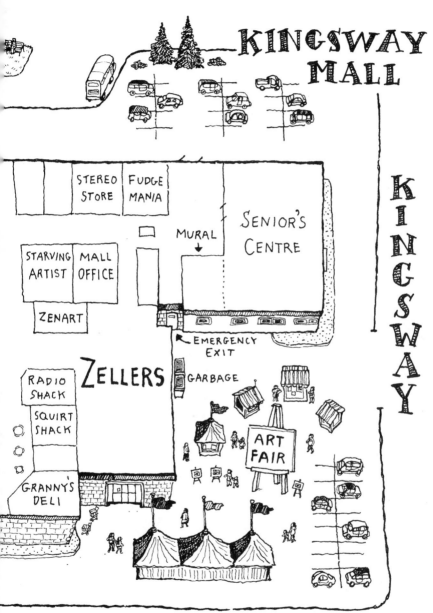

1. Invasion

"POLLY, IF YOU DON'T DO SOMETHING ABOUT YOUR room, I will!" Polly's mom stood in the kitchen, hands on her hips. Jan McDougall, fitness instructor and neat freak, glared at her daughter.

Polly blushed to the roots of her reddish-blonde hair. Not a good time to come home from the swimming pool, she thought, as she untied her sneakers and put them on the shoe rack by the front door. She didn't know which way to look – right at her mother's red face, past her trim athletic body at the tidy apartment, or toward the closed door to her own room. "I'll clean it."

"You'll need a shovel, if you ask me."

"Yes, Mom." Polly tried to sidle down the hall past her slender mother, blonde and tanned from her summer's running and outdoor exercise classes. But her mom moved in front of her and opened the door to Polly's room, ignoring the "Do not enter on penalty of dire consequences" and "Stay out, that means you" signs in orange and black felt marker on grey paper, complete with doodled rabbits top and bottom.

"I moved your clothes from the floor to the bed. I

found three glasses, a mug, and a cereal bowl hidden under a pile of jeans. You used to be such a tidy child. What's happened?" Her mother's voice was shrill.

"I said I'd clean it up, okay?" Polly felt blood rush to her head, her ears burning, her hands shaking. "It's my room."

"It's our apartment," her mother shouted. "Don't forget that, young lady."

Polly bit her lip. She wanted to yell back, "As if you'd ever let me forget!" But she didn't. She didn't like fights, especially with her mom.

"What's all the racket?" Polly's big brother Shawn came out of his room. "Oh, it's the lazy, thoughtless kid routine. Lighten up, you two, I'm packing for hockey camp." He stood between them, surveying Polly's room. "Oh ho, the new Edmonton dump site, I see."

"Shut up, Shawn," Polly muttered. Her muscled, curly-haired teenage brother leaned against the door frame and chuckled. "Been there, done that," he said. "You need to negotiate for space, Polly. It's one of the rules for big kids. Didn't you know there's a whole new set of rules for teenagers? Get with the program! I've settled somewhere between chaos and order – with no dirty dishes 'cause that freaks Mom out. Right, Mom?"

The chill in the hallway had disappeared.

Jan McDougall did a couple of knee bends against the wall. "I'm going for a run, Polly. When I get back, I want your room tidy."

She grabbed her water bottle, strapped it into its orange neon pouch, and disappeared through the door. The smell of toast and cinnamon came wafting in from one of the apartments down the hall.

George, Isabel Ashton's wire-haired terrier, woofed from behind his apartment door as Polly's mom ran down the stairs. His cheerful bark reminded Polly that she was not alone, not the Mistreated, Misjudged McDoodle after all. She had friends like Isabel, the retired art teacher, in this apartment building – and a big brother.

"Thanks, Shawn," Polly said. "You saved my ashcan."

"Mom's pretty good, but she has a couple of 'hot spots,' you know. Keeping the place clean and neat is one of them."

"Right."

"She's worried about leaving you alone while I'm at camp."

"I'll be okay. They're only going to Red Deer for a wedding, for Pete's sake," Polly sighed. Her mom hovered over her like she was some little kid.

Polly backed into her room and nearly tripped over a discarded sandal. All her clothes were piled on her bed, even the stuff she had aimed at the laundry basket and missed. She'd have to work fast.

Polly moved a heap of socks and plopped on the edge of the bed. I feel like the Invaded and Insulted McDoodle, she thought. Like a bird protecting its nest, I don't want anyone touching my stuff, my space. Not even Mom. My stuff is part of me, it tells me who I am. She picked up a bright blue cow T-shirt and sniffed it. Clean. She put it in the second drawer.

She sighed, grabbed her hairbrush from the floor, and brushed unruly hair away from her smooth, roundish, not-too-bad but not gorgeous face. Then she went about the tedious job of sorting underwear, shorts, and T-shirts into the right drawers or the laundry basket. Books went on the pine shelf, CDs in the rack, art supplies on her desk, stray drawings in her in-basket, trash into the bucket by the door.

She opened the window to let in warm summer air, let out the mixed odours of old socks, crackers, and stale dill pickle chips. A siren wailed on Kingsway, reminding her about the apartment building's next-door neighbour, Mr. Payne, who had been taken away last week in an ambulance. It seemed strange to have the old stucco house dark most of the time. She wondered whether hospitals would let twelve-year-olds in to visit heart attack patients.

Looking over toward the old willow tree in the parking lot, she nearly dropped a book on her foot. A strange boy was hammering a sign onto the railing of the tree fort. Some bratty, ugly, younger kid with straight black hair and porcelain pale skin – some kid Polly had never seen before in her life was setting up housekeeping in their private place. "Hey, kid, get down. Now!"

Polly dashed from the apartment, down the stairs, and flew out the back door, across the asphalt to the base of the willow. "Get down, if you know what's good for you." She shook her fist at him.

The boy stared down at her from the top of the rope ladder. He had knobby knees with scabs, worn black sneakers without socks, jean shorts two sizes too big, a wrinkled, stained T-shirt, startlingly grey-green eyes, and a mouth rimmed in purple Kool-Aid. "Who says?"

"I do. It's our fort. You're trespassing. Only the kids

in this apartment building are allowed."

"I moved in. So it's mine, too. My dad says." The boy blinked.

"Who's your dad?"

"He's Peter Bianco, the artist."

"Big deal. I'm an artist, too. Get down," Polly said firmly. "You aren't part of the club."

"Come up and make me, girl."

"You got a problem with girls?" Polly put one foot on the rope ladder and then another. The kid backed away from the edge. Polly climbed the ladder and pulled herself onto the plank floor of the fort. Her red plastic milk crate was dumped over. A couple of uncapped Magic Markers had rolled into the far corner. The kid had been using her markers to make his sign and standing on her crate to hammer it in. What nerve!

He stood by the railing, hands by his side, a big hammer gripped in his left hand, his face sporting a frown as wide as the North Saskatchewan River. He didn't say anything.

Polly leaned over the side of the fort. "Christopher's place," the sign said. The printing was lopsided and awkward. "You're no artist, that's for sure."

The boy grinned. "Never said I was. My dad, Peter, is the artist. He's Italian-Canadian with a dash of Danish thrown in for good measure. He says lots of Italians are artists. He works at the art supply store in the mall. Who are you?"

"You'll have to take the sign down."

"Why?"

"I told you. This fort belongs to us."

"But we live here. We moved in last weekend.

Doesn't that make the fort mine?"

"What grade are you in?" Polly tried her older-student-mentor voice.

"I'm going into Grade Three. I'm smart."

"Pretty sure of yourself, Christopher, for a little kid. Take the sign down."

"I just put it up. This hammer is heavy." He pouted. "It's my dad's. Can you lift it?"

"You can't invade other people's spaces, Christopher. Don't you know the rules? That's my crate. Those are my markers. At least you didn't touch Kyle's trunk."

"I couldn't figure out how to open it. Who's Kyle? Have you got a key? Can I look inside?"

"Don't even think it."

"Think what."

"Kyle Clay owns that trunk. He and I are partners in a business. This is our office, okay?" But there hadn't been any work for *McDoodle and Clay, Detectives* for a whole month. Not since the polluters of Small Shadow Lake had been caught. Kyle with his extra-logical mind and Polly with her doodling and poking around had helped the police solve the case. That was when Kyle nicknamed her the Intrepid Polly McDoodle.

So far, this summer had been pretty dull. Kyle Clay was at computer camp in Vermilion and Erin Darby, her once-reluctant and reticent neighbour and now close friend, was visiting relatives on a Woodland Cree Reserve up north. All Polly did was go to the Oliver pool, the playground, the mall, and art classes with Isabel.

"Can I join your club, can I?"

Polly shook her head. This kid was persistent. Like

Isabel's dog, George. A real terrier gnawing away at a bone or a piece of rawhide. George had played a major role in Polly's first real mystery.

She might just as well answer his pesky questions. "Kyle, Erin, and sometimes other kids use this fort. We all know each other. We don't know you."

"Yes, you do. I'm Chris. I live in an apartment on the third floor." He pointed to one of the third-floor balconies where a small barbecue and two white plastic lawn chairs sat. A pile of boxes filled one end of the tiny space.

"Nurses from the Royal Alex live up there."

"Not any more. They went somewhere else. My dad rented it from them, seeing as my mommy is away in Hong Kong. Hong Kong is a long way away. That's where my mommy's from. She's Chinese-Canadian. I'm an all-Canadian boy, my folks say, with a good dose of European and Asian blood. That makes me special." The kid talked non-stop. His left foot tapped as he chattered.

"We used to rent a house on the south side. Daddy can't pay for it. When Mommy comes back we'll get another house, I guess."

"Sounds pretty confusing to me." Polly shook her head and laughed. Kids sure tell you everything. Had she ever been that blabby? "How long are you staying?"

"I don't know. I don't know when Mommy is coming back." The kid danced up closer to her. "Can I play in your fort, can I?"

"You'll have to take down your sign."

The big frown widened. "I've always wanted a tree fort. It's neat. It's cool. I could sleep out in it, hide in it, you know. How long have you had it? Maybe we could build an addition, what do you think?"

"I'll ask the others. Most of the kids are away."

"Would you ask? For me? Right away, like soon?" He danced around her, so close she could smell lemon from his skin, or shirt. Polly backed away. He came closer. She backed away. It wasn't the smell. It was how close he stood. She needed an invisible space between her and anyone else, a private space. He was invading that. Polly fled down the ladder and across the parking lot.

"Until I ask around, you'll have to stay out of the fort, hear me?" She turned and looked at the kid in the tree fort. He was sliding his hand along the wooden railing like it was the fur of a precious pet. The fort's old weather-beaten boards and planks glowed in the sunlight. Dear old beat-up fort that it was, it perched in that ancient willow, giving safety and security and invisibility at times for children hiding there behind the waving fronds of green. The dancing branches helped kids feel like they were floating above the parking lot, above the busy ground where the rest of the world lived. A lump formed in Polly's throat thinking about how she loved that old tree and all the times she had hidden there. She had drawn sketches, played with Kyle the Clam, or planned adventures. Now younger kids were taking over. She called out to the boy, her voice husky as if she had a cold, "Get down, I said."

The boy scampered down the ladder, agile as a gymnast. "Okay. Christopher Bianco obeys. Most of the time anyway, you hear me?"

Polly hurried inside to finish cleaning her room. She wished Kyle would come home. They'd been best buddies since kindergarten. He'd always been the quiet, brainy, logical one. She was the noisy, emotional artist. They were good for each other. Or Erin. Erin had shown up last spring with her fishing hat. She had scientist leanings and a big sadness inside from losing her dad in a hit-and-run accident. Now Erin was in a better space.

Here Polly was, surrounded by busy adults and a dippy kid. She badly needed someone to talk things over with. Was her mother right, was she getting more difficult to live with? She certainly felt more emotional about things and she didn't always know why.

Polly took out her sketchbook and started working on a drawing of the tree fort and the willow tree. She didn't need to look out the window to see it. It loomed on the permanent video screen she carried around in her head. She'd check later to make sure she had all the details. For now it was enough to be drawing, feeling the pencil in her hand as she guided it, hearing the tiny scratch, scratch of the lead, smelling the sharp metallic and wooden odour of pencil shavings which curled in the old ashtray on her desk. She added a magpie to the bottom corner. She'd been heavily into magpies lately. They were a noisy, annoying bird, but for some reason Polly sympathized with them. She started to feel more like her old self, the Intrepid Polly McDoodle.

After supper she'd go over and help Isabel work on the mural she had been commissioned to do for the Seniors' Centre at the mall. When the grocery chain had pulled out, the owners had given one corner of the mall to the community. Now volunteer contractors were fixing it up. Isabel was doing the mural just outside the interior entrance. She'd won the commission. It had been a proud day for her and for Polly too.

Some people might think it strange for a kid Polly's age to have a friend who was retired. But Isabel was a neat person. She was stocky and solid with short grey hair and paint on her hands. She'd taught art in high school in Barrhead for years before retiring to Edmonton. Now she taught Polly and a few other young people drawing, just for the fun of it. "To keep my hand in," she said. Polly respected Isabel. She was a combination grandma, teacher and friend. Polly walked George for her, especially in the winter when it was cold or icy.

She'd go and tell Isabel about her exhausting confrontation with her mom and Christopher. She'd doodle more in her sketchbook, a picture of Chris the new kid. First, though, she had better finish cleaning her room before her mom came back from her run.

2. I'm Innocent

ISABEL WAS STANDING ON A SHORT ALUMINUM stepladder, painting sky. Her body leaned toward her work. There was intensity in every stroke the artist made. She turned as she heard Polly approach. "Hi, kid. Grab a brush." Her blue plaid comfy painter's shirt was speckled with paint of every colour. She laid the brush on the top of the ladder and climbed down. "Need you to paint grass. In the corner by the door to the fire exit. We've got a lot of wall to cover."

"Okay." Polly pulled her paint shirt out of the black backpack she had taken off her left shoulder.

She was just putting the shirt on when a mall security guard came running down the hall. "Isabel. Isabel. Did you see a couple of teenagers run past here?"

"What's the problem?"

"Someone knocked over a box of paintbrushes and spray cans at the back door of the art supply store. They stole some, I'm sure of it. Mall rats in black hats."

Polly stood gawking at the agitated man. His voice rasped like a saw. Her ears perked up at the mention of what might be a crime. She wanted to giggle at the thought of mall rats in black hats. She could feel a cartoon coming on. Her nose twitched like one of her rabbit friends. She cleared her throat to ask about the suspects.

"Did you get a close look at them? Do you have a good description?" she asked. The older man turned and stared at her. Polly's black backpack yawned open at her feet. It was filled with brushes, tubes, bottles and a couple of spray cans.

"Caught you red-handed, didn't I? Where did you dump your black hat?" The old guy grabbed Polly's arm. "Wait until the boss sees this. Even if those things were being hauled away, they were private property. How did you slip by me anyway?" He started marching Polly down the hall towards the administration office. Their footsteps echoed in the quiet end of one of Edmonton's busiest malls.

"Harold, wait! Polly's a friend of mine," Isabel protested. "She just got here."

"I'm innocent," Polly blurted. Her throat was hoarse. Her skin prickled.

"Innocent, are you? What are you doing with all those paints and brushes? Tell me that, missy."

"Those are my paints!" Polly found her voice. It squeaked like Kyle's but it was loud. "I'm helping Isabel."

Harold let go of her arm. He glanced up and down the corridor outside the Seniors' Centre. "Are you sure of that?"

"Yes, Harold, she's helping me." Isabel sounded exasperated.

"We've got real problems, Isabel – right here in the

mall," the man said. "I think there are gangs. Young criminals."

Polly took a deep breath and looked right into the older man's eyes. They were blue and cloudy; one looked kind of weepy and dull. His eyebrows were so thin they disappeared. She studied him carefully, her artist self itching to capture something of who he was, in a sketch – his pale, narrow face wrinkled like a raisin, his skinny white moustache drooping like overcooked spaghettini, his black name badge crooked, his narrow shoulders hunched, his knees bent, his feet turned in, his brown shoes scuffed. For a security guard, he looked as dilapidated as an abandoned house.

"Polly's no criminal," Isabel said clearly. "Get a grip, Harold."

"What was I to think? No normal kid would have all those things." He shrugged and lowered his head, making Polly think of a turtle pulling into his shell. His name should have been Franklin, like the turtle in picture books, not Harold. "If you say so, Isabel. Anything you say."

"I'm an artist," Polly said. "That's why I have all this stuff."

Just then there was a scuffle between two teenagers at the other end of the hallway. Harold nodded sadly and headed towards the ruckus. "What next?"

"Harold has been really depressed ever since his wife died," Isabel said. "Make allowances."

"Allowances," said Polly. "He accused me of being a thief. My mom just blew up at me because my room was a shambles. Some kid tried to take over our fort. Now this. What a day." The usually daring detective felt less like the Intrepid or the Invisible Polly McDoodle than she could ever remember. Oh, Kyle, where are you? She had a funny feeling there was a mystery brewing right here in her neighbourhood mall.

Polly needed to catch her breath. She sat on one of the green vinyl chairs inside the Seniors' Centre. The smell of fresh paint and disinfectant filled the air. Polly pulled out her sketchbook. She flipped to a fresh page. She'd been trying to capture a family of magpies and there were three fairly new pages filled with sketches. A giant magpie nest covered one page. She had read in the bird book that those big nests took up to six weeks to build. They had several entrances and covered a mud cup where the eggs were hidden. Magpies were bold and brassy birds who protected their young and their nests fiercely. She nodded to herself. Chris was just like a magpie. He wanted a nest. She sharpened her pencil and felt the tingly temptation of a clean page.

This time she did a quick sketch of Chris in the fort with his hammer and his wrinkled T-shirt. Then she flipped back to the full-page drawing of the fort. She added a rabbit at the base of the tree that reminded her of the elusive rabbit she had seen last winter. She shaded in the bark and put more detail on the drooping leaves of the willow. Their fort – it had been there as long as she could remember. She and Kyle had grown up with that fort. They'd painted it, added new floorboards when the old ones wore out, rebuilt the railing, and replaced lost rungs on the rope ladder. She had to admit that it was getting cramped and small. It barely held three of them at once when they sprawled on the floor playing Monopoly. She sighed, thinking about a time in the future when she wouldn't fit in the fort, when she wouldn't want to climb the ladder. She shut her eyes for a moment as if by doing that she could shut out the day when she and Kyle and Erin would have to give it up. Where would they hang out then?

The mall? Not a chance.

Meanwhile, up on the ladder, Isabel was humming Second World War songs as she painted. Every once in a while she'd break into song – "Coming in on a wing and a prayer," "Don't sit under the apple tree with any-one else but me," "Keep the home fires burning." She had a bunch of songs that she knew all the words for and sang over and over. Isabel had lost her fiancé at sea. He'd drowned when his convoy was bombed. War must be awful. Did they invent corny songs to get through it?

"Trouble with a mural," Isabel said, "it's hard on the arms. Tiring."

Polly nodded. Without thinking, she had finished the sketch of the tree fort, shaded in the one of Chris, and gone on to draw a picture of shabby Harold with his watery eyes. Finally she'd drawn Isabel up on the ladder.

Polly glanced at the mural. She was supposed to be helping Isabel by painting grass over in that far corner. She spotted a black and white magpie, black beak and all, painted there, close to the skinny exit hallway.

"I don't remember you putting magpies in your pre-liminary drawings."

"What magpies?" Isabel stopped painting and waved her brush in the air like a conductor waving a baton. "I don't do magpies. You do magpies."

Polly pointed to the far left corner.

"Okay, kid. When did you do it? You're teasing me."

"I didn't. I'm innocent."

"I believe you, but thousands wouldn't." Isabel climbed down the ladder and peered over her glasses, stood back. "No, it's not your work. It's better than yours, Polly. Whoever drew this was older, and has talent."

"Are you saying I don't?" Polly asked. Not another criticism. She couldn't take any more. Suddenly she felt like crying. "I thought you liked my magpies."

"A little tender, are you?" Isabel went back up the ladder. "Polly, Polly, perfection eludes us all. I'm sorry."

"Forget it." Polly felt tears threatening to spill. She picked up her backpack and slung it over her shoulder. She wasn't going to hang around being the Misunderstood, Underappreciated Polly McDoodle, let alone be accused of something she hadn't done by some old security guard. She headed to the exit.

She decided she wouldn't even go to see her dad, Ted McDougall, the manager at the Excel Sports store. She could have dug him out from behind the counter or stacks of high-priced runners, and gotten him to take her for ice cream. He loved ice cream as much as she did, but she didn't feel like ice cream.

Life was peculiar. Everyone was accusing her of some major or minor crime. She was responsible for the mess in her bedroom, but that was all. So she wasn't the best magpie drawer in the world. She was just a kid.

As she crossed Kingsway at the lights, Polly looked back toward the mall. What was going on? Was there a graffiti artist on the loose? Were there really mall rats in black hats? Was someone playing a prank on her, drawing a magpie? But why on Isabel's mural? The Confused and Confounded McDoodle went home. She'd phone Kyle tonight. Tell her detective buddy everything. See if his logical brain could figure out what was happening.

She thought of how tall Kyle had gotten over the last couple of months. His spiky brownish-blond hair was actually staying flatter, getting darker. He'd started wearing a tiny gold earring. So much for her nerdy buddy. He'd started talking more, paying some attention to what he was wearing, working out more than the logical explanations for everything. Kids change as they grow. She was changing, too – but what was she becoming? Shawn was right. There were different rules for teenagers. Too bad they didn't publish them in the back of an Archie comic or something.

A mystery to solve would really be good. But she had to make sure to remember what her parents had pointed out after the Small Shadow Lake mystery when she was nicknamed the Intrepid Polly McDoodle.

"We don't mind you using your head to sort and solve. But please be careful. We don't want you chasing criminals. It could be dangerous."

Finding a graffiti artist who copied her work wouldn't be dangerous, would it?

3. Phone Friends

"THERE'S SOMETHING FUNNY GOING ON." POLLY WAS talking to Kyle Clay on the phone later that night. "Someone painted a magpie on Isabel's mural."

"So when did you do it?" Kyle's voice was nearly drowned out by the racket of kids talking in the background. "Isn't that your latest animal?"

"I can hardly hear you."

"We're having a party to finish off computer camp. I made my own home page. I was thinking of making one for *McDoodle and Clay, Detectives.*"

"Sure. I guess so. No, maybe not. I have to think about that. Do we really want to advertise? I'm not convinced I want people bringing our business up onscreen. I'm feeling invaded – first Mom in my room, then Chris in our fort, finally someone draws a magpie better than mine on the corner of Isabel's mural."

"So should we let the poor kid use the fort?" Kyle asked.

"He seems pretty lonely. I could keep an eye on him."

"Okay by me," Kyle said. "But don't let him into my trunk."

"It's locked."

"Good," Kyle shouted over the noise of the party. "Any suspects in the graffiti problem?"

"Not yet. There's bunch of artists around though. Harold claims there are a couple of gangs too."

"Isn't the mall having an art fair next week? Maybe that's why there's a plethora of artists."

"A what?" Polly giggled. A plethora sounded like a relative to the platypus. "Does it eat a lot, your plethora? Can I keep it in my room?"

"Save it, will you?" Kyle sounded annoyed. "I'll be home in a couple of days. We'll talk then. Meanwhile you are on your own."

"Thanks a lot, buddy." Polly hung up. She jotted down the time on a pad on the table by the phone. Lakeland College, Vermilion, P.M. to K.C. 324-5666. She had to pay for long distance calls. Her mom wanted her to grow up being responsible. It wouldn't come out of her allowance for a month. Still she had kept her words to a minimum, just in case. The Responsible, Respectable McDoodle liked that.

The phone rang. Polly picked it up. Kyle must be phoning back. "Did you forget something?"

"What?" Erin's voice rang in the receiver.

"Sorry, Erin. I thought it was Kyle." Polly blushed. "He and I were just talking."

"I wanted to check in. I miss you guys." Erin's voice sounded forlorn. "I guess I'm becoming a city girl."

"Aren't you having fun?" Polly asked. In her mind's eye she could see her dark-haired, tall, thin friend Erin moving gracefully as a deer browsing in a quiet meadow. At Small Shadow Lake, Erin had played a key role in solving the mystery.

"The swimming is great. The relatives are fine." Erin sighed. "What are you up to?"

Polly told her about the spilled art supplies, the mall rats in black hats, and the mysterious magpie.

"Do you think the two things are related?" asked Erin. "They could be two unrelated incidents."

"You're right. I need something to connect the two, don't I?"

"When I get there – hopefully after the weekend if I can talk one of my uncles into driving to the city – I'll help."

"Great!" Polly listened as Erin talked about the problems of the toxins in the northern river basin and the soil erosion. She thought back to when Erin first showed up in the apartment building. How cold and aloof she had been. Now they were good friends. Even if the girl was a Scientist Extraordinaire, as Kyle had nicknamed her.

"Sounds like this next mystery has more to do with art than science, Polly," Erin said. "I've got to go. I'm spending my aunt's money on this call. I told her I was missing my friends so she let me call. She's a real softy."

Polly asked Erin about letting Chris into the fort. They agreed to let him use it for a trial period. If he mucked with any of their stuff he would be banned.

Polly hung up and started whistling a stupid war tune from Isabel's repertoire, "I'll be Seeing You." She decided to call it quits and go to her room. As she was opening her window to its widest point, she noted two flies on the screen trying to get in. "In your dreams," she said. Unusual noises came from the back lane. Her bedroom light was off, so she stood there in the evening dusk and listened and watched.

The floodlight on the parking lot revealed an interesting scene. Little Chris was bouncing on his sneakers and circling a group of young people that she didn't recognize. The big kids were busy talking to each other, ignoring Chris. Watching the energetic boy trying to get anyone to pay attention to him made her feel really sorry for him. A tall gangly guy who looked a little older than the teens and sported a trim black beard strolled along in the middle of the crowd. Like a swarm of bees around a hive, the group moved around him.

"Dad, let's go in the house. I'm hungry. Did we eat supper? I don't remember," Chris tugged at the young bearded guy's hand. "Can we play a game?"

A few more whispered conversations and the bearded guy wrapped his arm around Chris's shoulder and headed toward the back door. "Catch you later!" he said. "I'll just feed my kid a meal." Here it was bedtime and he was thinking of giving Chris supper? What a dad.

"Goodnight, Peter. Goodnight Chris." The group ambled down the lane, laughing and talking.

So little Chris's father hung out at the mall. Polly was sure she'd seen some of those older kids before. Was there a gang? She shook her head and turned toward her bed. There in her familiar room with all her favourite things around her, Polly felt pretty secure. Other people she met seemed to lead complicated lives – like Chris with his mom gone and his dad so busy he forgot to feed him, let alone keep an eye on him. It reminded Polly of when she had felt like her parents didn't really see her. She'd felt invisible, The Invisible Polly McDoodle. Not now, thank goodness. Now she felt as if everyone saw everything she did.

As she curled up in her funky Mickey Mouse sleep shirt under a pink sheet, she wondered aloud. "Maybe I'm just too innocent. I don't know the rules for being a teenager – any more than Chris knows how to be a middle-sized kid. We both need help."

She dreamt of magpies and gabby children in a giant tree fort.

4. A Wandering Sleeping Bag

THE NEXT MORNING POLLY'S MOM HELD OUT TO Polly a gigantic, ugly, yellow plastic bag with a sleeping bag rolled up in a ball and tied with an old running-shoe lace. "Polly, do me a favour and take this sleeping bag to the dry cleaners. Your brother needs it for hockey camp and it smells like dirty socks."

"Can't he take it himself?" Polly asked and then realized she was probably being lippy. "Sorry, Mom."

Her mother's frown cleared. "Polly, I'm thinking you should come to the wedding in Red Deer with us. I don't like the thought of you staying alone."

"Oh Mom, I'll be okay. Erin will be back by then. I can stay with her. Rachel won't mind."

"I'm not sure," Polly's mom said. "You're not old enough to be on your own."

"Mom, I'll be fine. I told you, Erin will be back by then." She grabbed the sleeping bag and left the apartment, the Hovered-Over and Hounded McDoodle.

Polly had wanted to run over to the mall anyway – to check on the mural and Isabel. She had to apologize for taking off so suddenly. Paint some grass. She could take another look at the magpie. See if the invading artist had left any other identifying marks.

First thing, she dumped the ugly plastic bag and tucked the sleeping bag under her arm. She could hear George whimpering down the hall, so she went down the back way and said encouraging things to him through Isabel's apartment door.

"I'll walk you when I get back, George. Go have a sleep."

"Who are you talking to? Is there someone in there?" The boy Chris came wandering down the hall. He was eating potato chips, dropping crumbs on the hall carpet. "Where are you going? Are you going to camp in the tree fort? Neat idea.

"Have you asked if I can use the fort? If I can use the fort, can we have a sleepover?" The kid stood so close and his voice was so high-pitched and fast that Polly's first impulse was to run for cover. Just being near him exhausted her.

"Yes, you can use the fort. But if you mess it up...." Polly was silenced as the kid grabbed her hands and danced a jig with her in the centre of the corridor. He reminded her of a rabbit on a pogo stick, all bounce and dazzle.

George barked furiously behind Isabel's door. He could hear all the commotion Chris was making and, as Polly knew, George liked in on the action. She'd have to bring him a doggie treat next time she walked by.

"It's a dog," Chris yelped with glee. "Someone has a dog. Is a dog allowed in the apartment? Could I get a puppy? A German shepherd?"

"Slow down, Chris." Polly told Chris about George

and the small-pet policy of the apartment building. She told him about her errand. "I'm going to the mall to get this sleeping bag cleaned. I'm not having a camp-out with you. It's not your fort."

The kid hung his head and leaned against the wall. "Oh, right!" He sighed like a mournful puppy dog. "My dad's out. I lost my key. Can I come with you? Sometimes my dad goes over to the mall to hang out with his friends even when he isn't working. Some of them are planning a surprise for him. I'm not supposed to tell him."

Polly shook her head. She couldn't believe Chris. He was so in your face. How could his father let him out on his own? He wasn't any more than eight years old.

He bounced on his untied sneakers like there were rubber balls instead of feet inside them. "Can I come, then, can I?"

Polly nodded. Chris dropped a pocketful of elastic bands on the floor. They both bent to pick them up.

"Aren't these the elastic bands from the front hall? The ones we save to give back to the mail carrier?"

"I took them. They looked like fun." He skipped ahead of her, out the door, across the parking lot, and into the laneway without a backward glance. He was flipping elastic bands in the air as he went.

"You don't just take everything you see," Polly announced these words to the empty hallway. Someone needed to take that kid in hand.

Polly followed Christopher to the mall, the sleeping bag cradled in her arms like a sleeping baby. The Motherly McDoodle mumbled the rules that any eight-year-old needed to know, the ones Christopher needed so desperately. *Respect people's private space. Don't take people's things. Don't blather.* Was there any way to help the kid? She'd keep a list of what he needed to know in her sketchbook. At least that was a start.

BEFORE SHE WENT TO THE CLEANERS, Polly took Chris to see the mural and showed him the offensive painted magpie invading the bottom corner. She put down the sleeping bag and her backpack, leaning them against a pillar beside Isabel's lunch bucket and artist's folio.

"I came to work," Polly said. "And to apologize for yesterday."

"I'm going to watch," said Chris. "Watch you paint and watch for my dad."

Isabel was still working on the mural of the Hudson Bay reserve sale that had won her the commission. Her brow was furrowed as she studied her sketch with its grid and then the wall where she was working.

"Polly, we're old friends. I understand. It's okay." She climbed her ladder gripping a brush.

"But I stormed off! I shouldn't have."

"I figured out what was going on pretty fast." Isabel grinned. "A word to the wise. Don't carry anger over one lost game into the next set. Applies in tennis and life."

Polly nodded. It was a good rule. "Thanks, Isabel." She put on her paint shirt and started painting grass.

"What are all those old guys doing?" Chris asked. "Is that an old-time painting? Were you there when it happened?"

"I may be old, but I'm not that old," Isabel laughed and looked down from her ladder. "Are you the young artist's kid?"

Chris nodded. "My dad says he was just a kid when I was born, that's why we can be buddies. So what's the story?" He waved at the mural Isabel was painting.

Harold, the security guard, spoke up. He had just come along the hallway from one of the emergency exits.

"In 1912 the Hudson's Bay Company sold off a bunch of its land here in Edmonton."

"Why?"

"'Cause people wanted it and The Bay needed money," Harold said.

"Why did they have all that land? Didn't they have stores? My mom bought my pyjamas at The Bay," Chris glanced down as if he expected to see them. Instead he had on the same ratty sneakers, T-shirt, and baggy shorts. "Do you go to Bay Day? We only buy stuff on sale, do you?"

"They started out with trading posts. They started out as the Hudson's Bay Company in the 1600s. After the flood of immigration, they opened up stores." Harold began talking about life in 1912 as if he had been there. Polly noticed that he didn't slouch as much when he was talking about history. Harold warmed to his subject like a dedicated teacher.

Listening, Polly got the giggles thinking about trading posts and whether they were like fence posts. She shook herself. Pay attention, she scolded. Don't be the Foolish and Frivolous McDoodle – you are a big kid now.

Harold explained the whole story to Chris. His sad face had brightened. "Around each post, the Hudson's

Bay Company was granted 1,000 acres. On April 12, 1912, they gave out numbered tickets. The bearer could buy a lot. Edmonton was growing. My dad was in line all night to get a ticket. The people in the front of the line got tickets with lower numbers and they got to bid on the best lots. Some guys sold their tickets to rich people. My dad had a number in the 70s. But...."

"Where's your dad now?" Chris looked around as if he expected to see him.

"He's been dead for thirty years. He was a young man in 1912."

"Did you stand in line with him? To get a lot to build a house? I used to live in a house." Chris's voice dropped to a whisper. His shoulders sagged. "When my Mommy was here...." His voice faded away. "Did you help your dad build your house?"

"I wasn't born yet." As he talked, Harold walked up and down in front of the mural like a tour guide in an ancient city. "Who would have thought of this as being a very interesting subject for a mural? All those people lined up, cooking their breakfast outside, sitting on camp chairs, playing cards, smoking, drinking, arguing, horse-trading or trying to trade spots in the line, shivering, bundled up because of the cool spring night."

Harold sighed, "This mall is built right on the street where the city laid streetcar tracks to take people to their new homes – good old Kingsway. My past is buried here under asphalt, buried deeper than my parents' graves over in the old Mount Pleasant Cemetery.

"Isabel won the chance to make the whole story come to life in this mural. I wish I'd thought of it. This is my story, not hers. My whole life is buried in this neighbourhood. I'm the only one left. Soon I'll be gone and my family name will be forgotten." His left foot dragged on the floor, making a swishing noise. "This should have been my job," he muttered, his face turned away from Isabel. Polly heard him though. He sounded like a bitter man.

"Harold, you're making me nervous, pacing up and down like that and mumbling. Haven't you got the whole mall to patrol?" Isabel asked.

Harold strolled off sadly, nodding his head like a flower in a strong wind.

"He entered the mural competition, you know," Isabel sighed.

"Can he draw?" asked Polly.

"Nice little country scenes," Isabel sighed. "But he's no artist. I haven't the heart to tell him. He's a bit of an Eeyore if you ask me, but I like him."

"He reminded me of a turtle."

"A pretty old turtle," Isabel chuckled. "He means well, does our Harold."

"Why don't you marry him?" Christopher asked. "He loves you."

"Don't be foolish, child." Isabel shook her head.

Polly added another rule for little kids to her list. *Don't make personal remarks* – didn't Alice in Wonderland learn that from the Queen? Chris needed to know that. It's an invasion of privacy. Funny, Polly thought. I thought invaders were big ugly dudes with muscles as big as baseballs. Instead this little kid invades with words – or his squirmy body. He nearly had his nose on the mural. He was so close to Isabel's leg he almost knocked the ladder over.

"Back off!" Isabel, the usually gentle artist, shouted. Chris hung his head like a wounded mutt. "Sorry."

"I brought Chris over to find his dad. He's lost his key."

"Kids!" Isabel threw up her hands in despair. "Frankly, I like big ones – like you."

"Thanks, Isabel." Polly turned to Chris. "I think we better leave. Isabel has work to do," Polly said firmly. "I'll take you to find your dad."

"My dad tried out for that mural. He lost out too," Christopher said. "He needs a big break to come his way. Being a starving artist is no joke. That's what he says."

"He's got a job, though," Polly said. The two of them headed toward the north end of the mall.

"The pay is pathetic, Dad says. Peter Bianco, the artist, is worth more. If he had won the competition, he could have gotten his van from the repair shop." Chris ran towards the art supply shop. "Then we could drive to Disneyland. We saw a movie about Disneyland. I'd like to go there with my dad. Maybe he could get a job in Disneyland, painting things. Is Disneyland close to Hong Kong where my mom is?"

Without a word of goodbye, the kid ran off. Polly had never met a kid like him. He seemed to think everyone was his family, every place his territory, everything his for the taking. Polly went back to the mural.

"That little boy has no boundaries," Isabel clambered down. "Are you sure you want to take him on as a project, Polly?"

"He's the one taking me on. He keeps showing up in my life," Polly sighed. "Too bad Kyle isn't here to spell me off."

A gang of teenagers raced down the hall towards the theatre, waving their mall purchases in bags above their heads, yelling at each other and laughing. Harold stomped by with a heavy green garbage bag, growling about noisy, thoughtless hooligans. One of the movie ushers – the one with the blue-dyed hair, a gold earring and dark glasses – came by pushing a cart with popcorn in big bags and a garbage pail with a lid. Polly noted his nametag. It said "Mike S."

Polly filled in some grass around the magpie. Then she helped Isabel by painting the yellow church. She began humming along with Isabel, the two of them making great progress. "Coming in on a Wing and a Prayer," they sang.

Chris came running down the hall with his dad, Peter, walking behind him. His father had an art folio and grocery bags filled to overflowing.

"Dad's taking me home. He's bought Chinese food. Some people paid him to draw a sketch for them. I'm starved."

Peter Bianco was over six feet tall and skinny. He wore black jeans, a black shirt, and a black vest with shiny black satin on the back. He had three earrings in his left earlobe and a black beard. Polly didn't say anything about having seen him with all his friends and Chris. On second glance, Peter did look too young to be a father.

"These are my good friends." Chris's voice sounded babyish when he talked to his dad. "Isabel is the artist who got the commission you wanted. Polly says I can use the fort. I can't make a mess, though. Right, Polly?"

"I'm glad Chris has found some friends." Peter shook hands with Isabel and Polly. "I'm pretty busy." He had long arms and hands that waved with each speech. Chris, of course, was hopping and bopping around. While they chatted about the apartment building and its tenants, Peter Bianco's glance strayed to the mural. Polly couldn't figure out whether he envied Isabel's choice as mural artist or was picking up pointers from her work. Soon the father and son headed for the nearest mall exit.

Polly took a break with a can of cola. She sat in the Seniors' Centre doodling on her page, shaking her head. The Bianco family was a small tornado all of its own creation. She drew another picture of Chris bouncing along beside Peter and wrote out rule number four under the sketch. *Don't make personal remarks.*

"He looks as gaunt as Ichabod Crane in that spooky tale about the haunted bridge, 'The Legend of Sleepy Hollow.'" Polly said this to no one in particular. Chris's dad, Peter Bianco, hadn't looked like a dad at all, more like an aging kid. Polly had a dad that looked like a dad. She grinned, thinking about Ted McDougall's muscular figure. He had a broad chest and wavy salt-and-pepper hair. He was nearly forty-three.

"Aren't you supposed to be doing something?" Isabel said from her perch. "I know I assigned you to draw people this summer but...."

Polly had been watching everyone passing by. Her sketchbook was open in front of her. She had Chris's dad looking like a scarecrow and Chris like a jumpy kid with big ears and an open mouth.

A black-and-white pencil-sketch magpie sat in the corner of the page scowling. She must have magpies on the brain.

"Yeah, I'm supposed to take this sleeping bag to the cleaners." Polly looked around. Her backpack was leaning beside the pillar, right beside Isabel's lunch bucket and portfolio. Polly's eyes searched the length of the shiny marble corridor.

"Where did I put it, Isabel?"

"What? Your head, oh my discombobulated friend?" Isabel laughed, climbed down from the ladder. She wiped her hands on a rag with paint thinner on it. The smell pervaded the air. "I've heard of absent-minded professors, but not absent-minded kids." She gave Polly a quick hug.

"I can't see the sleeping bag. I dropped it here while I was showing Chris the mural. I put it beside your stuff."

Isabel shrugged. "Don't see it. Sure you brought it?"

Polly nodded. She retraced her steps down the corridor. She stared at the magpie in the corner of the mural. She looked around the corner where Harold had disappeared with his bag of stuff. An empty skinny hallway with a fire door. "Emergency Exit," it said in bold red letters. A black magpie with a brilliant white chest and a strip of bright blue on its side, done with felt markers, was sitting on the "T" in the word "Exit." Polly walked right up to the magpie and stared at its beady eye. "Who are you?" That's when she spotted the initials on a corner of the white chest – MP.

She retraced her steps and knelt down by the magpie on the mural.

"What on earth are you doing, Polly?" Isabel asked.

Polly didn't answer. She had her nose nearly on the mural. Sure enough, there on the corner of the magpie's chest were the initials MP.

She'd have to call Kyle tonight. After she dealt with the next crisis in her short life. She had a clue, but she also had a big problem. Her mother was going to throw a hairy fit. Polly shook her head.

"Do you know an artist with the initials MP?" Polly asked.

Isabel shrugged her shoulders. "Not that I remember."

Polly picked up her small backpack and headed for the exit. "I've got to go home and face the music."

"What music?"

"Someone has taken the sleeping bag," the Besieged and Befuddled McDoodle moaned. "What is my mother going to say?"

"Probably something like 'You'd lose your head if it wasn't tacked on!'" Isabel laughed.

That didn't help Polly's mood at all. This was no laughing matter.

5. At the Pool

POLLY'S BROTHER SHAWN ENDED UP TAKING ONE OF her parents' sleeping bags to hockey camp. Her mother ranted at her all evening and half of the next morning about being careless, thoughtless, foolish, and too trusting by half. Polly's dad tried to be more understanding. It ended up with Polly feeling really guilty and sad. In desperation Polly left for the Oliver pool.

She was towelling off after a refreshing dip and a conversation with a couple of kids from her class last year.

"Hi, Polly." A flood of drips from wet hair cascaded on Polly's sun-warmed shoulder. The unmistakable giggle of Chris Bianco reverberated in Polly's ear. "My dad's got the day off, so we drove over in his van. He picked it up from the garage. He got paid. We'll give you a ride home if you like. His 'lost boys' are with him. That's what Mommy calls all his young artist friends. Do you know why she calls them that? Do you? She calls him a Peter Pan. Did you see the movie *Peter Pan?* Peter Pan wants to be a big kid his whole life long. My dad is like that. Sometimes he has to be grown-up, he says. I like it when he plays with me. He plays with the boys too. They play Dungeons and Dragons. Today they came swimming. All the boys are here. And Maeve. She's the short one in the dark blue swimsuit with her tummy showing. She's an artist too. She makes jewellery. See, she made me an earring." He shoved his face down close to Polly so she could see his big ear with the tiny little angel earring in it. "She likes me and sometimes she cooks real food for us. We have to do the dishes first or she won't go in our kitchen. I think she'd like to adopt us, but I told her we already had a mother. Maeve says we live in a dump. Do you think we live in a dump?"

"I've never been in your apartment." Do I need to know all this? Polly asked herself. All this information about a family that was probably going to disappear as suddenly as they appeared.

"You should come. The boys are nice. Mike gives me loonies to spend when he gets some. He's the thin one with the blue hair and big ears. He does cartooning and works in the movie theatre. He's an orphan, I think."

Polly remembered seeing Mike at the mall, wheeling garbage past Isabel's mural toward the emergency exit. "I have friends of my own, thanks." Polly thought about getting back in the pool, but Chris had plopped down on his towel right beside her. He smelled more like chlorine than lemon today. The scabs on his knees were all pink and shrivelled because of the water. He was shivering.

"You need to warm up before you go back in."

"I'm fine. I can stay in as long as I want. Daddy doesn't mind." Two seconds later he raced to the edge of the pool and leaped in. He was gone. Polly rubbed the side of her head behind her ear, as if to wipe away all the data Chris had just given her. She needed time to take it in. Mike was an artist and a movie usher with blue hair. Maeve made jewellery and was smaller-boned than Polly.

Polly folded her towel over her arm and headed to the other end of the pool, where Peter Bianco and his friends were tossing a tiny beanbag around.

"You're the kid in the apartment building," Mike said. He tossed the beanbag to Maeve. "You have a dog. I've heard him barking."

How come Mike knew so much? Did he live near the apartment? He had his information wrong though.

"No, Isabel, the artist, has the dog. I just walk George for her."

"Maybe you should get a dog, Peter," Mike laughed. "He could clean up the crumbs off the floor. It's cheaper than a vacuum cleaner."

"That's all you guys need," said Maeve, shaking her short, short black hair to dry it, and then speaking directly to Polly. "Chris says you're his friend."

Polly shrugged and studied Maeve closely. "I guess so. He's young, but he's persistent." The girl wasn't much taller than Chris, skinny as a stick, with pencil-thin eyebrows. She had a row of tiny earrings down each ear and one ring in her belly button. Her towel and her baggy shirt were black. Her glance kept flitting to Peter Bianco.

"Hey, we're all going to the mall after to sign up the boys as volunteers for Art in the Garden," Peter said. "I've got a gig as a street performer – doing balloon animals and caricatures. Do you want a lift?"

Peter and his son both talked in disconnected sentences, moving from one subject to another without a break. It made Polly dizzy, as if she were watching a ping-pong game.

"I just came over to say Chris was getting too cold."

"He knows when to get out of the water. Don't worry. I don't believe in hovering over kids." Peter glanced around the pool at the bouncing, splashing mass of humanity. Chris was nowhere to be seen.

"He's awfully young," Polly murmured.

The group around Peter was packing their towels, talking among themselves. There was Peter, Maeve, Mike, and two big quiet boys with blond hair, refrigerator-style bodies, baggy jean shorts and white T-shirts saying, "Get a life, why don't you!" They looked like twins. The group began moving toward the change rooms leaving a cluster of debris – discarded tissues, several Popsicle sticks, an empty french fries box, and a neat row of squished ketchup packets. Polly scooped up the garbage and dropped it in the nearby trash can. These guys suffered from what her mom would call dropsy – drop everything and run. I guess I can't talk, Polly said to herself – look at my room.

"Hey, you guys, where are you going?" Chris's voice rang out from the top of the slide. "Don't forget me, Dad. You didn't say you were leaving. Why didn't you say you were leaving? I like to know."

Perched on the top of the slide, yelling like that, the thin little kid looked frightened as a baby bird perched on the edge of the nest. He didn't seem to know whether to go down the slide or scramble back down the ladder. A gaggle of kids clustered behind him. Chris just sat there, his skinny legs dangling on the green slide.

"Make up your mind, kid," the lifeguard yelled. "Move it!"

Chris pushed off and landed with a splat in the water, then surfaced, spluttering and splashing. He clambered out of the pool. "Wait for me, Dad. Wait."

"Kid makes me nervous," one of the quiet boys said.

"Me too," the other one echoed.

"He's afraid that we'll leave without him, Josh, Bruce. He's just a little kid." Maeve handed Chris a towel.

"Are you coming too, Polly?" Chris beamed.

Polly hesitated. She didn't really know these people very well. What would her mom think?

"Can we give you a lift?" Peter asked. "We're going straight home. Save your bus fare for another day. Chris would be happy."

"We don't bite," Mike said.

"Not often," Maeve said, and slid her arm through Peter Bianco's. "Right, Peter?"

"Okay," said Polly. "I'll meet you out front."

"I'm glad." Chris jumped up and down. "Now I've got company." The smile on his face was broad as a hug. "Sit beside me. Sit beside me."

POLLY SAT IN THE BACK SEAT of the old van, strapped in beside Chris. Clutter littered the floor – discarded gum wrappers, apple cores, juice boxes, McDonald's french fries containers, more crumpled ketchup packets, a pair of black socks, a black ski hat. One dirty sneaker was jammed under the seat. Odours of old food mixed with gas and lemon air freshener. And Polly's mom thought she was messy. These guys needed help. Wow!

The radio played one of the top ten hits really loud. There was a speaker right beside Polly's left ear. She could barely think.

"Interesting collection of people," she whispered. "Wait until I tell Kyle."

"What?" Chris asked.

"Never mind," Polly said. "I'm just talking to myself."

"Do you think they'll let me be a volunteer? I'm nearly nine. I could be a gopher. Go for this and go for that. That's what my dad says I'm good at. What are you good at?"

Polly had been listening to the boys in the seat in front of them. Bruce and Josh were talking to each other. "It isn't fair. It's not as if we meant any harm," said Josh. "People have too much stuff anyway. The consumer society stinks."

Polly wondered why these boys were so mad.

"Too much stuff," said Bruce. "How were we to know it would break?"

"People shouldn't have stuff like that just lying around," said Josh. "Right in the open."

"Right in the open," said Bruce.

"Teens get blamed for everything these days," said Josh. He had a row of angry pimples on his cheek.

"Everything these days," said Bruce. His voice had an edge to it that made Polly shiver. "We'll show them." He took a ketchup packet out of his pocket, bit it open and drained it. Polly shook her head. Weird guy. Her fingers itched. She wanted to draw a sketch of these young people – the twins Josh and Bruce, Mike with his long nose and narrow face, and little Maeve.

"What are you good at?" Chris was leaning so close to Polly she could feel his body quiver from the cold. His pale skin was blue-tinged, his scabby knees were wrinkled, the scabs puckered like baby shrimp.

"You should get out of the water before you get that cold."

"I'm not cold," Chris's teeth chattered. "I want to know what you're good at. I think when someone asks a question you should answer it. I've asked you three times."

Polly ticked off another rule, number five for Chris: *Don't pester people.* "I don't know what I'm good at besides art. I'm no good at sports except swimming. I'm a dreamer. I have daydreams, nightmares, and night dreams. I make good chili con carne. My dad taught me."

"Do you want to know what I'm good at? Do you?" Polly sighed. "Sure."

"I'm a musician. I have a keyboard. I can play by ear. I'm going to be famous. My mom pays for my lessons. If she doesn't come back, I don't know what I'll do. What will I do? Do you want to come to my place and hear me play?" The kid was pulling the tufts on his towel. Polly wanted to reach out and stop him.

"Kyle is a musician. He might be able to help you when he gets home." He should be home by now, thought Polly. Relief was at hand.

"Will he like me? Will he?" Chris switched to picking at the scab on his knee. "Is he your boyfriend?" he giggled. Polly looked away.

"Just don't pester him too much. He's a bit shy," she said.

As the van pulled into the parking lot behind the apartment building, Clays' green 4 X 4 was backing out of its spot. Everyone climbed out and dispersed. Polly leaped from the van and hurried over. Mrs. Clay rolled down her window.

"Are you off to get Kyle?" Polly asked.

"We're picking him up and heading out to Small Shadow Lake for a few days."

"Oh, shooting matches!"

"Is something the matter, Polly?" Agnes Clay's forehead wrinkled.

"It's just, well, we may have another crime to solve."

"I'm afraid you're on your own for a few days. You could always come to the lake."

"Oh, no. It's all right. I'll be fine. I'm helping with Art in the Garden."

"Good." Agnes Clay buckled her seat belt. "Is Erin helping too?"

"She's up north with her family."

"I thought I saw Rachel with Constable Joe Haynes, the Mountie." The grin on Mrs. Clay's face told Polly how she felt about Erin's mom and her constant dates with the Mountie from Camrose. Erin was the only one struggling with their romance. Polly thought it was kind of cool watching two older adults, over thirty at least, acting like two teens in love. She didn't let on to Mrs. Clay though.

"Whatever." Polly turned and trotted toward the back door. Shoot, she was still on her own. It made her angry for a moment.

"Have a good time," she turned and hollered. The Clays couldn't hear her. They had driven off. Polly shoved the toe of her sneaker so hard at a clump of grass by the path that it flew into the air, leaving a gaping hole in the lawn. She glanced around quickly, bent down, and plopped the clump back into its place. The caretaker could get pretty snippy. As she raised her eyes, she could see the grey-painted box with electric wires in it that sat in the middle of the small patch of grass nearest the apartment building. A grinning magpie with a large berry in its mouth strutted on the side facing her. Squinting her eyes she could spot the initials MP. Shades of the magpie artist. What was he or she doing near Polly's apartment building?

She turned the key in the outside lock and opened the door.

"What kept you?" Chris asked. He was holding the inside door open for her. "We're all going over to sign up for the Art in the Garden. Come with us. Please. Hurry up."

This kid was sure persistent.

"If you don't come, who will I play with?" Chris's smile turned upside down. "The others are too big. They don't want me around. Not really."

Polly sighed. If her friends were going to desert her, maybe she would have to make do with Peter's weird bunch and this chattering kid. "Oh, all right! I'll be right down, I promise."

Her body felt sluggish, as if she'd just swum in mud instead of in a swimming pool. Summer was supposed to be the best of seasons. Instead she was feeling like the Abandoned and Alone McDoodle. She didn't know how to draw that.

6. Art in the Garden

POLLY STOOD IN AWE. TWO GIANT BLUE-AND-WHITE tents had been erected in the parking lot of the mall, close to the main entrance. A couple of long truck trailers were hooked up to generators. A van with steaming dry ice sat close by. An outdoor stage had been erected with banks of coloured lights and flags waving and huge black speakers blaring with mall music. What a transformation!

A table was set up inside the main doors close to the coffee shop. Two volunteers wore brand new Kingsway Seniors T-shirts. Harold, his uniform tidier than usual, stood guard behind them. He was brushing flecks off his left shoulder nervously. Polly had never seen such a bad case of dandruff. He should try one of those fancy shampoos they advertise on television all the time.

"What do you kids want?" he asked, eyeing Polly suspiciously. He still regarded her as a potential mall rat or a gang member, Polly figured. The Rambunctious and Renegade McDoodle – not very likely.

"We're here to volunteer," piped up Chris.

"You're too young, sonny," said a white-haired

woman with pinkish tinted glasses and a shiny pink tracksuit. Her sneakers were so white Polly wondered if they had ever been worn outdoors. Her name tag said "Hi, I'm Gladys. Can I help you?"

"I'm twelve," Polly said. "He can help me."

Maeve, Josh, Bruce, and some other teens were signing up with the other woman. Everyone was given a form to fill out. Polly took hers over to a table close to New York Fries and sat down. Some of the teens bought giant fries and grabbed a pile of ketchup and vinegar packets. The sounds of boiling fat, murmuring voices, mall music, and cash registers clanging, made a strange accompaniment to Polly's work. She licked her lips as she wrote. She filled in her name, address, and phone number. Under particular skills, she put "artist."

"Do you think you should put my name down on there if I'm going to be your helper? What's a helper do?" Chris bounced up and down beside her, waving a small flag he'd gotten off the table.

"Did those women say you could have that flag?" Polly asked.

"I didn't ask. I just took it. Why?"

Polly shook her head in despair. Rule number six for kids: *Ask before you take something.* "Go back and ask." She doodled a fast sketch of him waving his flag, put the rule under the picture. Chris did a little dance in front of her.

"Why take it back?" He bounced over, trying to get a look at what she was drawing. Polly covered the sketch up.

"What do you draw in that book all the time?" he asked. "Can I see it? Can I?"

"No, it's private property," Polly said. "Take the flag back."

"Why?"

"Because I said so. If you are going to be my helper, you have to co-operate with me."

Chris nodded about sixteen times in succession like one of those crazy dolls with its head on a slinky. The kid had springs instead of joints. He ran back to the desk and butted into line in front of everyone.

Polly sighed. Being a parent must be quite the job. She'd never thought about it much. For one second, she felt something like sympathy for her mom and dad. Raising kids was hard. As it was, she figured grown-ups had pretty boring lives, working and doing housework. If they were like her parents, they lawn bowled. They were into swimming, running, or watching hockey.

Chris came back in five minutes waving two flags proudly. "They gave me one for you too." The bright orange-and-green triangles of shiny neon fabric had white lettering that said "Art in the Garden" and sported the Kingsway Garden Mall's logo.

Polly took her filled-in application form over to Gladys. She was given a "Hi, I'm –. Can I help you?" badge, an Art in the Garden T-shirt, a pile of maps showing where all the exhibits were, including a schedule of events and shows, a list of performers, sponsoring groups, and businesses. She took a Magic Marker and printed her name on the badge.

"Report to Mr. Russell, the volunteer coordinator in the Seniors' Centre. He'll tell you what your job is." Gladys turned immediately to deal with a new applicant. Harold beamed at her as if she was a prize volunteer.

"I wonder what we're going to do? What do you think?" Chris skipped along beside Polly. He was blowing bubbles and waving the two flags. "Don't you just love malls?"

"Do I really want to take on this kid?" Polly asked herself again. Just because all my friends have abandoned me. She looked down at him. His skin was pale, almost translucent, like soapy water. I like him, in a funny way, she reflected. He's so innocent and trusting. Reminds me of myself when I was a kid. Maybe they were both innocent.

"You better stay outside while I get my assignment, Chris. As Gladys said, you're too young to be a volunteer. Some grown-ups get pretty sticky about rules. Why don't you visit Isabel at her mural? Tell her I'll be over in a jiffy."

Chris saluted like a soldier. "Yes, boss."

In a couple of minutes, Polly left the Seniors' Centre for the mural. There was a crowd milling around Isabel. Chris came running toward Polly. "Someone hit the church with a hammer. Someone smashed the church."

"What are you talking about?" Polly broke through the crowd.

Patrick Connelly, a police officer from the local station, was there. Polly recognized him from last winter when thieves had stolen the gifts and jewels from her apartment building.

Isabel was talking. "I just got here, Patrick. I worked late last night trying to get the mural finished. I wanted it done in time for the closing celebration of Art in the Garden week."

Harold handed her a glass of water. How had he gotten here so fast? Hadn't he been on duty right behind Gladys just a few minutes ago? If anything, the poor man looked more hunched over than ever, his head tucked in, his eyes darting over the faces in the crowd. "Mall rats. A gang of mall rats," he muttered. "I've seen mall rats in black hats."

Polly's fingers itched. She wanted to record the scene of the crime. The yellow church in the picture, the one where the land seekers picked up their numbers so they could get a chance at a prime lot, that small church had been smashed. The wallboard Isabel's mural was on looked like a giant fist had broken through. A splintered two-by-four showed underneath. Paint chips, flecks of plaster, hunks of wallboard, and strips of paper lay on the floor.

Isabel sat on a folding chair that the volunteer co-ordinator had brought from the Seniors' Centre. Mr. Russell carried another glass of water from his cooler. He smiled gently. Isabel was fanning her flushed face with a glossy advertising brochure.

Harold was talking to her, not in his solid history-telling voice but in a less sure, rambly chatter. "There, there," he said. "I guess you'll have to wait for this to be fixed. You can't work now. It's too upsetting. Maybe someone else should do this. I wouldn't mind helping. It might be dangerous for you, Isabel, my dear." He took a spotless white hanky out of his pocket and wiped his forehead. "The mall can't be responsible for your safety. But if I was working on the mural...."

"I can take care of myself, Harold," said Isabel. "You take care of the mall."

Harold looked disappointed. "It might help our

investigation if I were here. But whatever you say." Harold's face was very red. "We think there is a gang. They dress in black. But most kids these days dress in black, don't they? Who's bad and who's not, that's the question? I don't know what to do. You should let me finish the mural. I'm not afraid of them. No sirree!"

What was Harold going on about? Polly slid quietly over, nodded at Patrick who smiled as he recognized her. Polly stood beside Isabel. Harold didn't know Isabel very well if he thought a little vandalism would stop her.

"I want this repaired right away," Isabel commanded. "I've got work to do."

Harold's head bobbed. He sighed loudly but didn't say anything more. He disappeared in the direction of the mall office.

"Do we have to mount a guard?" Isabel asked.

"I could take a turn," said Polly.

"Me too," added Chris.

"Harold can help," said Isabel. "It's his job."

"This is beyond the mall security system's jurisdiction," Officer Connelly said. "Real vandalism is police business."

"Is vandalism a criminal offense?" asked Polly.

"Indubitably." The officer tugged his uniform jacket down.

"Who does nasty stuff like this?"

"Most acts of vandalism are pretty random," said Patrick seriously. "Frequently unhappy youths seeking a sense of community. Hard to catch the perpetrators."

Polly had to swallow a giggle. Kyle would have liked that word – perpetrators. She'd have to phone him tonight at his cottage and bring him up to date. She could tell him Patrick Connelly liked big words as much as he did.

"Someone smashed the bus shelter on the east side of the mall last night. No one saw anything," Officer Connelly said. "Incredibly difficult to investigate such random acts of violation."

Polly felt her detective's brain snap into high gear. "Could it have been done by the same people? Did they use a hammer?"

The policeman ignored her question and followed his own train of thought. "There has been an increase in disturbing incidents." Patrick's beeper went off and he headed towards the doors. "Call if you ascertain anything."

Isabel was grinning at Polly. "Talks like a dictionary. He and Kyle would get along well. Where is that boy when we need him, eh?"

"Speaking of boys, where's Chris?" Polly surveyed the hallway. The crowd had dispersed and Chris had disappeared with them. "I don't like an eight year old wandering around in the mall on his own," Polly said. Rule number seven: *Tell someone where you are going.* The Older and Wiser McDoodle sighed.

"He's probably gone to see his dad. Peter's at the booth by the art supply shop," said Isabel. "Chris's dad is a pretty good artist for a young guy. Hasn't really found his own style yet. Has to work, of course. Spends too much time with his young friends. Art takes concentrated effort over a long time."

"So do kids," Polly added. "Chris gets lonely. He misses his mom more than he says." She was thinking of how he had gone on and on earlier at the pool as if talking a lot would keep him warm and safe. The kid missed his mom.

"Are you talking about me, Polly?" Chris popped out from behind a kiosk in the centre of the hall. "Harold's coming with the repair guy. Maybe I can help."

"We're supposed to put these flyers on the cars in the parking lot." Polly took the gold-and-green flyers out of her backpack. "Don't dart between cars and get run over."

"I won't."

The two kids walked through Zeller's towards the exit.

"I'm glad we're working together. I can't believe I have a friend that's all grown up like you. Isn't growing up scary, Polly? How do you know how to act? I don't always know 'cause we move a lot. Maybe I can pick up some tips from you."

Polly wondered for a moment whether she should tell Chris some of the rules. Now didn't feel like the right time. She'd wait for a quiet moment. Besides, they had work to do. And she had some investigating to do as well.

"Wait a minute!" Polly said. "Let's start on the other side – close to the bus shelter. I want to see if there are any clues." She turned on her heel and headed down the corridor.

"Oh, boy, am I a junior detective now? Am I?"

Polly shook her head. "No, you are an assistant volunteer. I'm the detective."

"What do detectives do?"

"They detect." Polly's voice was brisk.

The kid frowned, shoved his hands in his too-big

jean short pockets, and slouched along beside Polly. "I just asked a question."

The two kids turned the corner by the popcorn kiosk and headed down the side hall past the Wizard's Lair with all its video games. An empty store across from the Wizard's Lair had brown paper covering all the windows – and a magpie on the top right-hand corner near a sign "Watch this space for an exciting new store."

A few older teens were playing video games. The two quiet guys, Josh and Bruce, were busy playing a game on a giant screen computer near the front of the Wizard's Lair. That couldn't be their volunteer assignment. Who were these guys? Where did they live? What had they broken that she had heard them talking about? What kind of art did they do?

Polly's detective muscles flexed. Whoever was drawing the magpies had access to the mall at odd hours when no one could see them working. The magpie artist was proud of his or her work, because the initials were on each drawing. Too bad they hadn't written their whole name the way Isabel did. But it was only initials like Polly wrote when she recorded a phone call. So the magpie artist wanted to be noticed but not identified – like a graffiti ghost.

"What do detectives do? I want to know." Chris was pouting.

"Detectives look for clues, talk to witnesses if there are any. They think about motive and the way things were done. They think about all the angles. They get a list of suspects. It's like doing a jigsaw puzzle." Polly pushed open the door to the parking lot.

Warm air struck her in the face like a splash of water.

The sun made her squint. She put on her sunglasses. Leaving the mall was like leaving the water after a long time in the pool. The world outside felt alien. She felt alien. Alas, the Alien McDoodle had work to do.

As they walked across the parking lot, a beat-up orange Volvo with a spray-painted dragonfly on the passenger side door nearly ran them over. The windows were tinted dark green but Polly thought she could make out four people. Loud headbanger music roared from speakers in the car. Polly shook her head and pulled Chris close to her. They ducked between two rows of cars. "Jerks!" she cried.

"Is that a gang of mall rats?" asked Chris.

Chris and Polly headed over to the bus shelter. Sure enough, two of the side panels had been smashed to smithereens. A repair truck with three men in city uniforms parked nearby. The men got out and started shovelling up shards of plexiglas, pieces of metal, and paper from the posters. Garbage from a tipped barrel was strewn around – plastic spoons, food scraps, empty poly cups, and containers. Busy magpies squabbled over torn buns and french fries. Stray mustard, ketchup, and vinegar packets were spread everywhere.

Sun beat down on the passengers waiting for the next bus.

Polly blinked fiercely, trying to record the scene so she could put it in her sketchbook later. One large lively magpie screeched from a telephone pole, another from a light standard. She could see their giant nest hidden in the spruce that towered in the centre of the sea of cars. Weren't the baby birds worried by all the noise of the parking cars, the car exhaust, and now the repair people? "They'll be gone soon," she spoke to the birds. "Enjoy your feast of junk food."

"You are weird. I don't know anyone else who talks to birds," Chris said. "Do they understand? Do they?"

Polly sauntered over to the shambles and peered inside.

"Watch out, kid. That could be dangerous," one of the repairmen called. The metal bench that had been in the shelter stood empty in the blazing sun – except for a small magpie painted on its surface, a magpie very much like the one on Isabel's mural, very much like the one by the emergency door in the mall and the one on the electrical box outside the apartment building. "MP" was written in black Magic Marker beside it.

The question formed in her mind – was the magpie artist the vandal as well? Many people caught buses here. There were too many suspects and too many clues – like a magpie drawn on the bench, and litter everywhere from the smashed shelter.

Polly couldn't tell what had done the damage. It might have been a hammer, but she had no way of proving that. She stood frowning. Was the magpie artist responsible, or did she or he just take the bus from this spot?

"Are you coming, Polly? It's too hot," Chris asked.

"Okay. I wanted to check out the scene of the crime." She didn't tell Chris about the clue. "Put flyers on car windows. That's our job."

Polly moved to the first line of cars. Halfway down the row she discovered an ancient tank of a car with smashed windows and headlights. The back bumper was missing altogether. Who would do a thing like that?

Two tiny brown sparrows pecked at food scraps on the front seat. They fluttered up and then returned to their feast as she came near. She didn't put a leaflet on the poor car. She knew cars were not as important as human beings, but they were sometimes precious to their owners. Someone might be really sad about this. She shook her head, thought of how precious some of the places and things in her life were; the fort, her room, her sketchbook, her favourite pens. The Protective and Pensive McDoodle backed away from the vandalized heap.

She moved quickly to the next one, a red Honda Civic. She touched the shiny hood with her fingers. "Boy, the metal body is hot. Be careful."

"Too bad they can't air condition the parking lot," Chris laughed, a funny kind of hiccupy laugh. "Do they have air conditioning in Hong Kong? Mommy doesn't like it too hot or too cold. She hates Alberta winters. Her daddy's sick. Mr. Li. He's dying, I guess. She's staying with her mom. If he had gotten sick in the winter, then she would have missed the cold. Does it take a long time to die?"

"It depends."

"Oh!" He looked at all the cars and people in short-sleeved shirts. Some had floppy hats to protect their heads. "I don't like it real hot, do you? Do you like cold or hot better?"

Polly shrugged. This kid had a mouth as wide as the North Saskatchewan River and it ran nearly as fast. "I prefer hot. I'm always losing mitts and I hate wearing snow boots. My mom insists on snow boots."

"So does mine. When she's here. Dad doesn't notice

– he's an artist. He forgets his mitts himself. He might forget me too, he's so absent-minded." They talked as they lifted windshield wipers and stuck the papers under. "I'll be late for school every day if I go with my dad. What will I do? Who will pick me up?"

"It's a long time until school starts."

"I like to know what's happening," Chris sighed. "I get really worried."

"Sometimes we can't know stuff," Polly said.

"I wish I knew...." Chris was getting red in the face. Polly didn't think it was from the heat.

"Don't worry so much."

"Everyone tells me that. I don't like it," Chris whined. "Mommy said I was to be a big boy while she was gone. Sometimes that's hard."

"Maybe your mom will come back soon." Polly tried to sound encouraging and friendly.

"It doesn't matter." The kid gave her a really disheartened glance. "I don't need anyone. I don't need anyone at all. Why should I need anyone?" Chris darted across the lane and started stuffing papers on cars in the next row. Then he skipped across the parking lot to the mall entrance and disappeared inside. Polly finished two more cars and hurried after him.

As she was holding the door for a young mother with a stroller, she could see a wad of flyers sticking out of the garbage receptacle just outside the glass doors. She let the door close, walked back and rescued the papers.

Rule number eight: *Finish what you start.*

She was tempted to let the kid fend for himself. He was moody. He had a father. It was none of her business. She just lived in the same apartment building.

Polly trudged along the glass and marble hallway with its brightly decorated storefronts. Tables and displays of local artists, potters, jewellery makers, sculptors, and craft makers lined the centre of the corridor. Bright colours, interesting shapes, unusual textures surrounded Polly. She felt invaded again, only it was a joyful invasion, and made her feel bubbly inside. The artists were dressed in funky clothes and stood beside their work. A hum of excitement and busyness filled the mall.

Polly spotted Officer Connelly strolling along, talking to one of the volunteers. She mentioned the run-in with the old Volvo with the dragonfly on it. Then Polly told him about the smashed car. He shook his head in despair and headed out the door towards the wreck. "Even if the car had been abandoned, that's an illegal act."

Polly was left strolling through the group of strangers who moved in and out of stores. They sat on benches, sipped coffee, or licked ice cream cones as they walked along the teeming corridors. The fresh smells of popcorn, cinnamon buns, and ice cream mingled in a strange stew. Art in the Garden was in full swing.

Three teenagers Polly didn't recognize passed her. They were wearing baggy black pants, black T-shirts, and of all things, black ski caps on their heads in the middle of the summer. Polly smelled dirty bodies, gasoline, and oil. Long earrings dangled from each teen's left ear. She stared at those. They looked like dragonflies. They couldn't be real, could they? Don't be silly, Polly. They're shiny silver. How had the jeweller done the transparent wings?

Two of the young people were tall and one was skinny and short with tiny feet, and moved like a dancer.

They were headed away from the Wizard's Lair, jingling change in their pockets. One had a key ring as big as a two-dollar coin, with at least twenty keys of various sizes. He was twirling it in his hand.

"Move over, kid," the tallest said. "We own this mall. We're the Dragonflies."

Polly shivered, as if someone had walked on her grave. Her heart beat wildly.

She turned quickly to the bright lights of the Disney store at the corner. Polly talked for a few minutes to one of her dad's friends. He was busy stocking a display of Winnie-the-Poohs in the window. What a contrast! Winnie-the-Pooh and dark dragonflies in the same hallway. If they were dragonflies, who did they think were the mosquitoes they were out to catch? She shook her head to dispel the frightening vision of giant dragonflies and people as mosquitoes being eaten alive.

She chatted for several minutes with the Disney manager about their families, vacation, swimming, and the latest thing, the art festival.

"Should be a treat for a young artist like you, having Art in the Garden all this week?" the guy said, grinning.

"Yes," Polly replied.

"Should mean good business for the mall too."

"Dad hopes so." Polly moved on.

A mall is a small universe, she reflected. Her dad worked here. Polly had grown up knowing her way around his store, all the ins and outs of opening and closing, deliveries and shipping, security measures and customer care. Hundreds of people worked in a big mall like this one. Most of her father's friends were shopkeepers. Sometimes she worried about them all living inside all the time away from the sun, the wind, the grass and trees, and the birds. Some kids seemed to hang out at the mall all day and half the night. Security must chase them out before they locked the doors. Where did those kids go?

Polly could only take so many hours of life in the mall. She needed real sunlight and fresh air. She needed silence. Was there such a thing as noise pollution – music you haven't chosen, people you haven't invited, sounds you haven't made? A mall was a shopper's world, but Polly wasn't much of a shopper. The Puzzled, Pondering McDoodle made her way back toward the Seniors' Centre.

Three store lengths ahead of her, Chris was walking with one of the quiet boys. Must be Josh, because he was talking and he had zits. All Bruce did was repeat. Should have called them Pete and Repeat. Funny ha-ha, Polly. She was sure missing Kyle with his clever remarks.

Polly caught up to them on sneakered feet. Maybe that's why they talked about detectives as gumshoes – they needed good feet in silent sneakers. Would gum really help, or just make you stick to the floor?

"Listen, kid. If you want to be part of it, you have to promise to keep quiet about what's going on. Understand?"

"Did you like the pipe cleaner man I made for you, Josh?"

"Sure," the big boy glanced down at the bouncing eight year old. "Stop changing the subject. Now, what about keeping quiet?"

"Anything you say, Josh. I can keep secrets. I didn't tell

Dad about his Christmas tie last year. Mom made me promise and cross my heart." Suddenly Chris tripped over a shoelace and nearly took a header onto the brown-speckled marble floor, right beside a palm tree in a big pot. Polly took that moment of confusion to interrupt.

"Hey, guys, where are you going?" She thought of the wad of flyers in her backpack and wondered whether to tell Chris off. He stood there, eager and smiling, jiggling and wiggling between Josh and her.

"I got tired of delivering flyers," Chris said. "I left them. I saw Josh and ran after him. He's my friend."

"I thought you were helping me."

Chris hung his head and dragged a sneaker on the floor. "Sorry."

Finish what you start, Polly thought. That was one of her unwritten rules. It wasn't just meant for Chris and his dropped flyers. It was meant for her. She needed to help this kid if she could. The Mothering McDoodle, who would have guessed it? Certainly not her own mom. "I think you should finish what you start."

"Who made you boss?" Josh stared at her in a funny way, his eyes narrowed.

"Nobody," Polly said. "I'm just trying to help." She wasn't going to take on this big boy. He seemed angry.

She ducked down the next corridor, "See you later, Chris." Was there a ninth rule about choosing your friends wisely? How did little kids figure out whom to trust? She wasn't sure she trusted Josh or Bruce, let alone Mike, the blue-haired usher, or Maeve, the pixie-like jeweller.

She went and hung out in her dad's store. He smiled and waved as she strolled through the store to the back door. A mother with two teenagers was trying to convince them that they didn't need name-brand sneakers. Polly put shoeboxes back on shelves in the back room. When her dad came into the back for two boxes of Size-10-narrow runners, she gave him an impulsive hug.

"What brought that on?" he chuckled. "Not that I mind, mind you. I like it loads."

"You're a good dad," she muttered into his shoulder and went back to work sorting shoes. Then she went out and delivered the rest of the flyers, tucking them innocently under people's windshield wipers.

7. Too Many Suspects

"SLOW DOWN, POLLY," KYLE SAID. POLLY HAD TAKEN the cordless phone into her room after supper and called Kyle in Small Shadow Lake.

"Sorry, I guess I get carried away."

"The question is – are they random acts of vandalism like Officer Connelly said, or is there something else going on, something planned by a gang?"

She had already told him about the bus shelter, the car, and the hole in the mural.

"Do you have any suspects?" Kyle asked.

"Too many," Polly said. "The mall is crowded with artists and people who do crafts. There are tables with brightly coloured skirts along every corridor. The huge blue-and-white nylon beer tent they erected on the parking lot is out of bounds for us kids, of course. The tent is shaped like a nomad's tent from the deserts of Arabia. Only it's on a mall parking lot in Edmonton. I keep expecting to see a man in a flowing gown on a camel galloping up to it."

"A desert pirate? What an imagination."

"I'm just saying there's no way to narrow the investigation down."

"Who do you suspect?" Kyle persisted.

"There are some suspicious characters, but there are a couple of gangs of kids too – the Dragonflies and the young artists that hang around with Peter Bianco."

"What about the artists who submitted designs for the mural?" Kyle paused. "Could one of them be jealous of Isabel?"

"That doesn't explain the bus shelter or the car." Polly took a sip of her lemonade. She nibbled one of her mother's Rice Krispie squares. She would have preferred a peanut butter cookie, but it was summer and Jan McDougall didn't heat up the apartment any more than necessary. Polly mopped her forehead.

"That could be a copycat crime," Kyle suggested. "Someone who saw the mural and went and did the bus shelter."

"Or vice versa," Polly said. "We don't know which happened first."

"Can you find out who submitted designs?"

"I know two of them – Harold, the security guard, and Peter, Chris's dad."

"Find out who else."

"How?"

"Go to the mall office. Someone there should have a list." Kyle cleared his throat. "I better go. My dad wants to use the phone."

"Okay."

"I'll phone tomorrow night. Good hunting."

"Bye," Polly said.

Polly was sorry she couldn't discuss things with Kyle face to face. She liked going over everything a couple of times. Detective work took a lot of concentrated thinking – and drawing. She did a lot of doodles while they were working on a mystery. She should look at her sketches again. Kyle always looked at her drawings and made stupid comments about her reasoning ability and her maps. He made lists. It was a friendly rivalry though. She teased him when he clammed up and wouldn't talk.

Polly pushed papers into a pile on her desk and took a large drawing sheet. She began to make a map of the mall. She'd spent her whole life living near the Kingsway. Surely she could draw it from memory.

She was tempted to put a small human being, a little Chris, in the corner of her mall map. Only that afternoon, they had taken a break and gone for snacks. Chris had bounced around visiting everyone he knew – friends of his father, and then Polly's dad, and his new assistant. A group of four teenagers had come into the food fair area. The two that Polly didn't recognize sat at a table while Josh and Bruce went for french fries and drinks.

Isabel, Polly, and Chris were splitting a pizza. Chris, of course, was gallivanting, munching as he visited. Isabel and Polly had been working out how many hours they thought it would take to finish the mural. Isabel had a notebook out and Polly was doodling as they talked. She had finished sketches of Maeve, Mike, and the twins, Josh and Bruce. She'd drawn the orange Volvo with the dragonfly on the door.

Harold came marching in and walked right up to the two teenagers sitting at the table. "What are you wait-

ing for?" he asked snidely. "Christmas? There's no loi-
tering allowed here."

Just then Josh and Bruce, who had trays of food and
drinks, returned to the table. Josh took one look at
Harold's puffy face, slapped the tray down, and stormed
away. "That's harassment, that is," he said out loud. "I'll
show you." His brother Bruce followed him.

Isabel spoke up. "Harold, those boys weren't doing
anything wrong."

"You don't work in a mall like I do, Isabel." He came
over, but slowly, after he had made it clear to the group
of young people that they better watch their step. "Mall
rats. I know them when I see them."

"We were the ones using a table after we had finished
eating," Isabel waved her hand over the papers and
notes she and Polly had spread around them. "Are you
going to shout at us?"

"Of course not," Harold said, his voice softening as
he spoke. "It's those kids I can't stand. They're sloppy,
inconsiderate, and boorish. They need to learn table
manners. We didn't behave like that when we were kids
growing up around here."

Isabel's forehead had turned red, right to the roots of
her grey hair. "Harold, those kids were just eating in the
food fair. That's what it's here for, isn't it?"

Polly lowered her eyes to her page of drawing and let
the two older adults talk. She was thinking about what
it was going to be like, being a teenager. Harold grouped
all kids over twelve into one mass of badness. He used
his position to attack kids. No doubt there were some
bad kids in the mall. Maybe there were some bad adults
too. Her dad had a couple of McDougallisms about giv-

ing everyone the benefit of the doubt and trusting people until they proved untrustworthy. He believed most people were good. So did Polly.

"Lighten up, Harold."

"You don't know the half of what we security guards see." Harold glared at Isabel. "Vandalism, littering, bad language, graffiti – most kids are young criminals and I know what I'm talking about."

Isabel stood, collected her papers, and motioned to Polly to join her, walking back through the crowded mall to the mural. "I don't like prejudice in any form."

"I know," Polly said.

"Harold's becoming quite the grumpy old man," Isabel said. "I'm disappointed in him. I've made allowances."

"Uh-huh."

"It makes me sad and mad at the same time."

Polly just nodded. They went back to work, painting sky and grass. Chris tagged along. He washed paintbrushes and put them in jars according to size, whistling TV commercials as he worked.

Polly hadn't forgotten the scene with the teenagers. Sometimes at school a few of the kids would get mouthy or sloppy and get into trouble with teachers. She herself had been accused of talking too much. Not all kids were, as Kyle had pointed out, troubled teens or addled adolescents.

Chris took off to see his dad. Isabel decided to work through supper. Polly knew she had to get home.

On her way out of the mall, she spotted Maeve talking to one of the jewellery makers who shared a booth with a potter. Maeve looked like a pixie in her black outfit, her hair so short she looked like a young boy. She was showing the jeweller samples of her work and waving her arms dramatically. Polly figured all artists had to be pretty pushy if they wanted to get their work displayed. She didn't know if she'd be able to do that. Kyle would say she'd have to. But he didn't know how shy she felt some days, the Reluctant and Reclusive McDoodle.

When she got home, her father was making his famous coleslaw. Her mother was tossing hot pasta with egg, bacon, and Parmesan cheese – *spaghetti carbonara* she called it. Polly told them all about Harold, Isabel, and the teenagers as they ate supper.

"I know one almost-teenager I really like." Her dad pushed her bangs out of her eyes. "I can't see you ever turning into a mall rat."

"The ones that do don't get enough fresh air," her mother said. "Why not come for a long bike ride with your folks? We're heading down to the river valley, taking cookies and juice." Jan McDougall was busy tying her blonde hair into a ponytail and sticking her head into a bright yellow bike helmet.

"Have a good time," Polly waved them away. "I've got some drawing to do."

POLLY WAS BUSY SKETCHING the whole block the mall was on when she heard a commotion in the back lane. She put down her pencil and ran through the apartment and out through the patio doors onto the balcony.

"Chris, come down out of there!" Peter Bianco's voice was loud.

"I'm staying here." Chris's voice sounded whiny and babyish.

"You can't stay out here alone all night."

"Who says?" came the childish reply. "I'll be fine. I'm a big boy. Mommy said so."

"Mommy's not here. Come on in."

"You guys are going to spend the evening making too much noise playing Dungeons and Dragons," Chris whined. "You won't let me play with you, watch television, or play computer games. I won't have any fun."

"Christopher Bianco, come on down."

There was a long silence.

Mike came striding across the parking lot. His blue hair shone in the early evening sunlight. "So you finally found him. Hiding in the tree fort, eh?" He had changed out of his movie usher outfit and was wearing black cargo pants and a black sweatshirt with a flying hawk stencilled on it. Polly wondered where Mike lived. He kept showing up in their back lane.

"Chris ran away while I was working at the mall. Right after we'd had burgers and fries," Peter said.

"You were going to work. I came home," Chris whimpered. "I moved out here 'cause I wanted to, 'cause I knew you had a game tonight, 'cause I...."

"Chris is all right, Peter. He's a cool kid," Mike said. "I know what it's like, wanting attention. It's hard to get enough of it when you are a weird little kid. We all like attention."

Peter Bianco sat down on the electrical box just below Polly. She had been standing listening to the conversation. The Invisible Polly McDoodle.

"I don't have eyes in the back of my head. I can't keep

up with him. I've got work and my own life. Chao says she can't come home until her dad dies. I can't afford to send Chris to Hong Kong."

"What about your family?" Mike asked.

"They live on the East Coast. Mom and Dad both work and don't like kids much."

"I know what you mean," Mike said. "I left home when I was sixteen to become an artist. My dad wanted me to be a lawyer. My big brother is one. I'm the family disappointment."

"Working in a movie house isn't being an artist," Chris hooted from the tree fort. "Where's your art – in the dark halls?"

"Quiet, Chris," Peter Bianco said. "Mike draws great cartoons."

"Are cartoonists artists?" Chris asked.

"Not according to my parents. Cartooning isn't a profession in their eyes. I worked my way across the country, doing odd jobs. I'd like to settle down, you know. Artists need the company of other artists. That's why I hang out with Peter and the gang." Mike sighed. "Sometimes I get lonely, though."

Polly heard a note of sadness in Mike's voice.

"Why Edmonton?" asked Chris. "Why not Disneyland or Hollywood?"

"I've an uncle, a retired pipefitter. He lives here in Edmonton. I think he'd understand," Mike pushed his hair out of his eyes, "but nobody answers his phone, or his door, and there's no answering machine."

So where was this kid living, Polly asked herself? She hadn't paid much attention to the comings and goings in the back lane lately. She'd been too busy over at the mall.

Mike was still talking. "So I understand how Chris feels."

"I don't see the connection," Peter said.

"Turnabout is fair play. Maybe Chris doesn't want to live 'an artistic life.' He's just a kid. He wants a normal kid life."

Polly watched as Peter Bianco put his head in his hands. "I didn't mind being a daddy at nineteen. I was excited. I didn't know how much work raising kids was. I'm not even thirty yet. Life's not much fun these days."

"Can't you find someone to keep an eye on Chris, at least during the Art in the Garden festival?"

"I can't afford to pay much. Babysitters make nearly as much as buskers."

"I could watch him for you," Polly said out loud.

"What?" Peter's head snapped up. He turned and looked up to Polly's balcony.

"I heard the commotion and came out to see who it was. I didn't mean to eavesdrop. Sorry."

"Polly, is that you?" Chris's voice piped up from the tree fort.

"I don't need a lot of money, a couple of dollars an hour would do," Polly said. "I could buy some neat things for school."

"Sounds like a win-win situation," Mike said.

"What about your mom? Will she say it's all right?" Peter asked.

"Is Polly going to be my babysitter, is she?"

"I have to check, but Mom will say it's fine." Then Polly had a brainwave. "Chris, if you come down from the tree fort and go with your daddy...I'll promise to have a sleepover in the fort the last night of the festival. How's that sound?"

There was a loud crash as the milk crate fell over, a scurrying and a scrambling. Chris appeared at the base of the old willow tree, his Star Trek sleeping bag draped over his arm. "It's a deal."

Polly skipped down the steps to talk to Peter Bianco. In a couple of minutes they had outlined plans for the next few days. Polly promised to talk to her mom when she came home from her evening out with Dad.

"We'll start tomorrow when your dad goes to work. I'll call before that if there's a problem."

Polly went back to her drawing of the mall and the streets around it. She doodled rabbits and magpies around the edges.

She made a list of some activities she could do with Chris and a bit of a schedule in her sketchbook. She wrote out the list of her nine rules for successful kid life – in case she had a chance to do some subtle training. She wanted to add one more – a tenth rule, something about believing in yourself. Every once in a while Chris got all confused or angry when he didn't know what was going on. He needed more confidence.

When Kyle came back, maybe together they could train this kid to be more responsible and confident. The Subtle and Suave McDoodle undressed and got ready for bed. She had her first real job. Was this the end of innocence?

8. A Family Resemblance

"SO WHAT ARE WE GOING TO DO WITH THIS KID?" Kyle asked, nodding in the direction of Chris, who had decided to travel at the back of the bus, staring out the back window. Kyle's family had finally come home from their cottage on Small Shadow Lake. McDoodle and Clay had had quite a debriefing session in the tree fort and later that morning on the bus over to the swimming pool. "What's the plan?"

"We need to keep an eye on him. Maybe help him with his music," Polly answered. "I admit I sometimes forget about him. I'm not used to being responsible for others."

"I understand." Kyle took off his thick glasses and began to polish them with a small baby blue cloth. Still the nerd, thought Polly, even if his spiky hair was so short it didn't stick out. His jean cut-offs displayed long, thin legs, rumpled mismatched socks, and seedy sneakers. His nose was peeling and the tips of his big ears were red. Still it was great to have her gawky friend back. Maybe when he was sixteen he'd be a hunk, who could tell?

The bus snorted as it pulled to the stop closest to the pool and the three kids got off. Exhaust fumes billowed in the air. Kyle coughed.

Kyle and Polly shared an old army blanket on the grass beside the Oliver pool. Chris played with a couple of other eight year olds in the shallow end. Laughter and squeals of delight rang out loud and clear in the bright hot air of a fine summer day.

"Yesterday I took him with me when I helped the Seniors clean up the outdoor stage between performances," Polly lathered on more sunscreen. "He dropped as much as he picked up."

"Were we ever like that?" Kyle tossed some of his sunflower seeds toward the fence where a real magpie teetered. The magpie flew down and scooped them up.

Polly figured that question needed no answer.

"I helped him clean his room the day before yesterday. I found a letter he had written to his mom. It had a yellow sticky note on it, 'Please send this, Dad.' Her e-mail address in Hong Kong was posted on another sticky note on the monitor, so I copied his note onto the computer and sent it. Peter told me not to let Chris on his computer, but he said he trusted me. I doubted Peter would ever get around to sending that message. Peter's a really nice funky guy, but not really attentive to household chores or details in his son's life."

"What did Chris say to his mom?"

"Normal stuff about what he was doing, where he had been, how much he missed her. Something weird about the coffee gallery nearly being ready to open. He'd written a line about running away if she didn't come home. I didn't know whether I should copy that. If her dad is dying, she doesn't need any more worries."

"Tough choice."

"I included it."

"My parents never let me out of their sight when I was his age. I thought they were strange," Kyle flopped over on his other side. "Overprotective."

"Mine were the same."

"Chris seems awfully nervous and jumpy, anxious to please." Kyle wrinkled his forehead like a professor with a problem. "Maybe it's better to have parents at you all the time when you're little."

"I don't know. Mom gets angry pretty easily."

"My dad gets so wrapped up in work he forgets to talk to anyone," Kyle said. "Who can figure adults out? It would take better detectives than us, that's for sure."

"Speaking of detectives – I copied the list of the names of the people who submitted entries for the mural commission. There were five local names – Massimo Peter Bianco, Harold M. Palmer, Isabel Ashton, Michael Payne, and Gladys Bongard. One entrant was from St. Albert, a Bruce Springstune."

"Catchy names."

"Three of them are MP's, like my graffiti ghost – Massimo P. Bianco, M. Palmer, and Michael Payne," Polly said. "The question is which one is the villain."

"Or are there more than one? Is it really a gang?" Kyle asked.

"We have the funky artists with Peter and the Dragonflies. Then there are the mall rats in black hats, as M. Palmer – otherwise known as Harold, the security guard – calls them."

"Harold, the security guard. I haven't met him yet."

Kyle munched on seeds. "Let's get back to the list of artists."

Polly read them out again.

"I can understand why Peter doesn't use his first name. Massimo is too much. In Italian it means the biggest. I wonder if the guy from St. Albert is for real. Sounds like a pseudonym, a play on Bruce Springsteen, the singer-songwriter."

"Where do you get all this trivia?'

"For a committed musicologist, that's not trivia."

"A musicologist are we, whoop-de-doo," laughed Polly. "That's something you can do with Chris – give him some keyboard lessons. Keep him out of my hair."

"I want to see that list you've got. Names, addresses."

"There's a short description of their proposed murals. I didn't see the sketches, though," Polly sighed. "They couldn't find them. They'd been planning on mounting them on a display panel in the front part of the mall, but they didn't look too good after the break-in, they said. I asked, 'What break-in?' The mall management thought I was being a nosy kid. They told me their office door had been broken and the office trashed. Nothing valuable taken. Vandals again. The night security guard reported seeing a small group of dark figures with black ski hats, that's all."

"Something funny is going on," Kyle muttered. "I don't think this is random. It sounds premeditated."

"Ooh, boy, here we go. Big Words Clay is at it again. Premeditated."

"Stow it, Polly. Figure it out. Someone thought this through and acted on their plan."

"Okay."

"The question is why? What was the motive?" Kyle scratched his head, making his short hair stick out funny. It reminded Polly of how he had looked in kindergarten when they first met.

"Was there any incriminating evidence?" Kyle asked.

Polly shrugged her shoulders. "Who knows?"

"What are we going to do now? What are we?" One damp and shivery Chris danced around the blanket, scuffing it as he waltzed. "Dad gave you money for ice cream, didn't he? I want it. I'll bring you some if you like. I like chocolate ripple. What do you like? We have to go home after this, don't we? Can I walk Isabel's dog?"

Kyle and Polly gazed at each other, over at Chris, and up at the sky. "Oh, brother!" they said in unison.

"Solving a mystery is much easier," said Polly.

Kyle nodded. He pressed his lips together as if maybe his being quiet would rub off on Chris. Polly watched the two of them move towards the boys' changing room.

THAT AFTERNOON the three of them went to the mall. Chris visited his dad as Peter entertained children and parents with balloon animals. Kyle took a turn at the electric piano in the music store. The owner wanted him to play more, because folks kept coming in to hear him and check out the prices. Polly handed out brochures to people as they passed the Art in the Garden booth near the entrance. She watched for strange people, but nobody showed up with black ski hats or wild looks. It was disappointing.

When she had a break, Polly wandered past the television store. A weatherman was warning that a series of summer storms was moving across the prairies. The news commentator hoped it would miss Edmonton and not ruin the Art in the Garden festival.

The vandal attack on the mural had been repaired. Isabel was working furiously because of the delay. Polly asked Mr. Russell if she could be assigned to help Isabel finish the mural in time for the final celebration on Friday night. The volunteer coordinator said, "sure thing," and grinned at her, showing off his white teeth. Polly produced her paint shirt and supplies.

"Should I paint over the magpie?" Polly asked.

"I've gotten used to him being there," Isabel said. "He's not doing any harm. I expect there were lots of magpies in Edmonton, even in the old days. We had more ravens in Barrhead. Noisy devils they are. More caw than calamity, thank goodness."

Polly worked on a cloud that hung over the yellow church. She used pure white and mixed it with tinges of blue and eggshell. It wasn't as bright as Harold's hanky or folded as neatly. In fact, the cumulous cloud looked as if a storm was brewing in the east. A couple of hours and this bunch of people might be in quite a windstorm. Funny, when you were painting a picture, how ideas of what would happen next came into your head.

Why would someone bash in a mural? What did they think would happen? That Isabel would stop working? That the mural would be ruined? That someone else would have to take over?

Motives are hard to discover, Polly thought. She tried to put herself in the shoes of the Random Vandal. What would drive an artist to vandalism? Jealousy because I didn't get chosen to do the mural. Anger because I think I'm a better artist or have a better idea. Or had the attack just been plain unthinking, unfeeling violence against things or people? I'll show them. I'll show them all. If I can't get attention doing something good, I'll do something bad. Polly scrunched her forehead in deep thought.

Her cloud was turning from puffy to more ominous. The darkness in Polly's head was transferring to the mural.

"Hold on a minute, Polly," Isabel called from below. "Aren't you getting carried away with that cloud? The weather wasn't that bad."

"I was thinking about motives. Who would do these things and why?" Polly looked sheepish. "I'll fix it. The guy on the television was saying there's a band of summer storms coming."

"Your fierce cloud is a product of the power of suggestion," Isabel chuckled. "The Easily Led or Over-imaginative McDoodle."

Polly ignored the comments. She was too busy thinking things through. "The person who vandalized might not be the one who had the motive. They might have just been going along with whoever wanted it done and got carried away."

"The Graffiti Ghost is definitely a good artist. An MP." She leaned her hand against the dry part of the mural. "The vandal could be one of the unsuccessful artists. But that doesn't explain the attack on the car, the mall office, or the bus shelter...."

"What on earth are you talking about, Polly?" Isabel asked. "If you are so busy detecting, you better climb down off that ladder. I don't trust you when you get dreamy."

LATER THAT EVENING, after Chris and his dad had gone home to their art-laden apartment, Polly and Kyle patrolled the area near the mural. Polly's dad had promised to bring them super-duper double-scoopers from the ice cream shop as soon as he closed the store.

Maeve came by. She stopped to be introduced to Kyle. "Have you seen Peter?" she asked Polly. "He and I had a date, I thought." When she mentioned Peter's name, she blushed, Polly noticed.

"He's gone home with Chris."

"That kid takes too much work. I thought you were watching him." Maeve sounded peeved. "Peter gave us your numbers to call if we were looking for him or Chris." Maeve nodded curtly at the young detectives. "I'll hang out with my other friends then." She hurried off.

"So that's Maeve," said Kyle.

Polly didn't say anything to Kyle, but she thought Maeve had a crush on Peter Bianco. Only Peter didn't pay as much attention to her as she wanted. Polly was glad. After all, he was married and had a little boy. Maeve should find someone her own age.

The mall was quieter than Polly could ever remember. Harold had passed by twice. Gladys, the older woman in the pink flashy track suit, who had worked at the volunteer desk when Art in the Garden opened, had been following him with bags of garbage on a trolley. Ever since Isabel had been busy with the mural, Gladys, her white hair permed, her white sneakers spotless, and her pink-tinted glasses polished, had shown quite an interest in shabby Harold. Isabel had cooled toward Harold because he was so grumpy. He needed someone to cheer him up, that was for sure.

Josh and Bruce came thundering past, following three other teens that Polly didn't recognize. Both boys ducked behind someone – as if they didn't want her seeing them. The whole troop ran toward the mall entrance by the Senior's Centre. That was funny. When Josh and Bruce were with Peter, Maeve, and Mike, they seemed friendly enough.

Polly pointed after the running twins. "Now you've seen the whole gang, Kyle," Polly said. "What do you think?"

On a table just inside the doorway to the Seniors' Centre, the two young detectives, Kyle and Polly, spread out the map and their list of mural artists. Polly's sketchbook was open.

"What do we know so far?" Kyle took his sharpened pencil and wrote on a clean sheet of paper.

"Magpies have been spotted all over," Polly moaned.

"The question is, are they related to the crime or just a red herring?"

"More like a black-and-white bird than a red herring," Polly said. "I really want to know who's drawing them."

"I spotted one on the garage door of old Mr. Payne's place next to the apartment building." Kyle took his ruler and measured the length of the mall in inches as he talked.

"I wonder what his first name is?" Polly stared across the table.

"I haven't seen him for ages," Kyle said. "There's a light on his back porch. It could be on a timer, right?"

"He's in hospital, you know," Polly commented. "I saw the ambulance pick him up. I wonder if he has someone watering his plants and mowing his lawn. I haven't been paying a lot of attention." She didn't want to talk about the fact that she had spent very little time in the tree fort lately, watching the neighbourhood for puzzling activities.

"It's too bad he's sick. Poor Mr. Payne." Kyle sighed, and erased a faulty line on his map.

"Where have I seen the name Payne lately?" Polly asked.

"On the list of submissions." Kyle picked up the list. He began reading the backup description for the Michael Payne submission aloud.

"'A mural about the flora and fauna of Edmonton. Using acrylics and paint, the artist will produce a beautiful scene of the river valley of the city, with the skyline and samples of all the flowers and animals who live in the city. Included would be moose, deer, coyote, muskrat, beaver, mole, vole, as well as birds like sparrows, hawks, peregrine falcons, owls, magpies, and robins. Signed Michael Payne.' The address is 11020 - 109 Street, Edmonton. That must be Mr. Payne, our neighbour. I didn't know he was an artist."

"I didn't either. He worked in the oil patch. He came back to live in his house after his tenants left this spring," Polly said. "Remember, they were the guys who raised flowers and we thought they might be growing marijuana." That had been last year when she and Kyle had helped solve the robberies in the apartment block before Christmas.

"They were innocent, just like you," Kyle laughed. "Presumptuous kids we were."

"Indubitably." Polly shoved Kyle's arm, making him scribble across the page. Kyle ignored her.

"When did Mr. Payne go into hospital?" Kyle asked.

"While you were away. He had a heart attack."

"So, he couldn't have done the mural anyway. He's off the list of suspects, that's for sure."

Polly stared at the description of the mural and the name. "MP. Don't forget, that's the initials on the magpies."

"Michael Payne. But he couldn't have done them either. He's in hospital."

"He could have done them before he went."

"Not the one on the mural itself," said Kyle. "Use your head. That didn't appear until last week."

Kyle stared at the list. "We have several MPs. Massimo Peter – if he went by his first two names. Harold Palmer's middle initial is *M*, so it could be him. Is Gladys Bongard his new lady friend? What does it say about her entry?"

"'The artist would make a piece of fabric art representing the golden wheat fields, an oil derrick, a grain elevator, and an expanse of blue prairie sky to celebrate the essential elements of the thriving economic benefits that surround our city of Edmonton. Materials used would be quilting, weaving, appliqué and collage.'" Polly shook her head. "How would you decide which entrant to choose."

"What was Harold's entry?"

"'The painter will do a panoramic picture of the skyline of Edmonton from a photograph taken by a special camera.'"

"Sounds boring," Kyle said.

"It would depend on the portfolio of previous work, and the credibility of the artist. Real artists have a wealth of experience," Polly said proudly. Working with Isabel this past year had taught her quite a bit. It was one area where Polly felt pretty sure of herself.

"Peter Bianco planned 'a futuristic view of the city as in 2200, done in bold graphic design.'" Kyle sharpened his pencil.

"Michael Payne proposed magpies." Polly doodled one on the edge of the paper.

"But Michael Payne is in hospital."

"And he's a pipefitter."

"Could someone else be using his name?" Kyle asked.

"That sounds too complicated."

"Definitely," Kyle said.

"What about Bruce Springstune? What did he propose?"

"He wanted to do a three dimensional photograph with real things stuck on it – like violins and guns and beer bottles and books," Kyle reported. "The city as commodities and consumerism."

"Sounds freaky."

"Fairly *avant garde* and abstract," Kyle murmured. "*Tout chez* trendy."

Polly chuckled. It was so good having Kyle back. No one else she knew talked like him. It was comforting. Of course, sometimes he didn't talk at all. But when he did he used language like a blanket, wrapping up ideas in neat parcels.

"I <u>know</u> why Isabel won. She's a better artist and she had an interesting historical idea as the focus. Besides, she's my teacher." Polly left the table and wandered out to take a look at the mural.

Isabel was standing in front of it, hands on her hips. "It's done." She did a little twirl. Polly figured this mural let Isabel show off her skill. It was pretty exciting.

Polly and Kyle joined Isabel and admired the finished product.

"I hope I can learn to do faces like you can," Polly said. She pointed to a young man in a cap and breeches halfway down the line of waiters. "Is that Harold's dad? Did you use Harold as a model?"

Isabel shrugged and grinned. "Maybe."

"Who's this guy?" Polly studied the thin face and big ears of one of the old fellows toward the back of the line. He was eating a sandwich and sipping from a tin cup. "He looks familiar."

"That's Mr. Payne's grandfather."

Polly and Kyle stared long and hard at the face of Mr. Payne. "We should go and see him in the hospital. Maybe we could take a picture of the mural so he could see his grandpa's face."

Polly wrinkled her brow in thought. "He looks familiar."

"It's the family resemblance," Kyle said. "Of course he looks like Mr. Payne."

The man in the tweed jacket was skinny with a long thin nose. He had a cleft in his chin and large ears. His head seemed narrow, like someone had put it in a vice. "That's not who he reminds me of," Polly murmured. "It's someone I've seen recently, in the last few days."

"I think it's time we went home." Isabel said. "Tomorrow I'm sleeping in."

Polly and Kyle gathered up their materials, shoved them into Kyle's briefcase and Polly's backpack. Isabel took one last look at the mural. Then she pulled the curtains that had been erected to cover the finished mural so that it could be unveiled at the closing celebration.

Harold's evening replacement let them out the emergency exit closest to their apartment block. "I'll keep an eye on the mural tonight," he said.

Raucous sounds came from the beer tent. The stage was silent. Even the magpies in the trees had gone to bed.

Tomorrow the mural would be unveiled and Art in the Garden would close. Polly was looking forward to the close of the show. She was getting tired of being a volunteer and of keeping an eye on Chris for his dad. I guess I'm not ready to be the Totally Responsible McDoodle yet, she mused.

Erin Darby was due back from the northern Alberta woods tomorrow. She'd called last night as Polly was getting ready for bed. She could help them with the problem of the Random Vandals and the Graffiti Ghost. She could sleep out in the tree fort with them. Polly's mom was relieved that Polly's friend would be home while she and Ted were away at the wedding.

The Determined and Dedicated Detective McDoodle closed her sketchbook and headed home with her buddy Kyle, leaving the night security staff to keep an eye on the mural. Maybe overnight some clues as to the identity of the vandals would show up. Polly hoped so.

9. Cleanup Time

THE NEXT MORNING KYLE AND POLLY WERE IN Chris's apartment helping him tidy up. Polly had brought George the dog. Isabel had gone shopping for a new outfit to wear at the unveiling of the mural that afternoon.

"Boy, do I like having a dog around." Chris bounced around the living room after George and tossed socks rolled into a ball for him to chase. George barked gleefully. He hadn't had this much attention for months, Polly figured.

George sniffed every chair and every stray pillow. He ate spilled popcorn, a pizza crust, and a lone red-and-white striped peppermint he found under a couch cushion. He hauled a black ski hat out of the front hall closet. Polly grabbed it from him. So Peter Bianco had a black ski hat. There had been one in the back of his van too. Could he be a mall rat in a black hat? Who else?

Kyle was trying to get Biancos' Internet connection on-line. "It doesn't seem to be working. Neither the phone nor the computer will co-operate."

"The phone hasn't rung all day. All the young artists

check in with Dad," Chris said. "We usually hear from Mom too − she e-mails every other day. She'll worry if she can't reach us."

Polly was unloading the dishwasher and putting plates away. "Take the garbage out, Chris. It's overflowing. You need to recycle your tins. There is a compost bin and a recycle blue box in the backyard."

"I'll take the dog with me." He snapped George's leash on and grabbed the green garbage bag, then scurried out the door.

"The phone line is dead," Kyle said. "That's the problem. There's nothing I can do about that. Besides, I should go and get Brutus and take him out for a walk with Chris and George. I forget how much Brutus likes romping around."

"It's okay. I saw your dad walking him earlier. He was whistling. I guess he likes getting out too." Polly wiped the counters from breakfast and put the cereal boxes away. "Babysitting Chris has been a real eye-opener, I'll tell you. I must have been raised in a sterile environment. I can't believe these guys. The apartment smells like dead socks and unswept carpets. Yuck. Housekeeping sure isn't high on their priorities."

"My mom would have a fit," Kyle shook his head. "It's amazing." He started tidying up the spilled magazines, carrying dropped clothes to the hamper in the bathroom, and toys to Chris's room.

"And my mom calls my room a mess. She's as innocent as I am." Polly put a Scrabble game away on the top of an overcrowded bookcase. "I hope Chris's mom doesn't mind."

The two of them knelt on the rug picking up stray

coins. The McDougall cellphone rang. Kyle answered.

"Hello.... Who is it again?.... Oh, hi, Maeve.... I'm Kyle, Polly's friend. You and I met last night. What?.... Yeah, he's with us. Peter's working at the art supply store today, said something about picking up art in his old van.... Polly, Chris, and I.... The coffee's on.... I'll tell him."

"Who was it on the phone?" Chris came through the door waving a piece of paper with a magpie on it. "See what I found at the base of our fort."

Kyle grabbed the paper and stared at it, passed it to Polly. Then he responded to Chris's question.

"That was Maeve. She said the coffee is on. Do you know what that means?"

"Yeah." The kid beamed. "Maeve and the lost boys have talked the guy who is opening the small café at the end of the mall into putting up a display of Peter's art. It's a one-man show. That's some big deal for an artist. We've kept it a secret. I didn't tell Dad. They made me promise. Just like I didn't tell him that the boys broke that statue Mom had on the mantel."

That must have been the statue Josh and Bruce had broken. The way they talked it was as if it was Chao Li's fault for putting it on the mantel. Crazy mixed-up kids. Did they have a different set of rules than Polly?

"Why the secret?" Polly asked. "Won't your dad be pleased?"

"Yeah, but he said he wasn't ready. I let the boys and Maeve into the storeroom in the basement so they could make a selection of his best work. Maeve took them over to the mall in her old beater of a car. She really likes Dad a lot. But he told her last night when she came over late, he told her that he was happily married, that they would just have to be good friends. I don't think she liked that. She's been sounding grouchy ever since. She yelled at me. But she's still helping with the art show. Now my dad can get the attention he deserves." Chris's voice broke. "I'm the only one in the family who nobody..."

"Who nobody what?" Polly asked.

"Never mind." Chris ran from the room. George, the dog, followed. The apartment door banged behind them.

"Kyle, can you sleep out with Chris and I tonight? I promised him a sleepover in the tree fort. I don't really want to do it all on my own. My folks are going to a wedding in Red Deer. They made me promise to keep in touch."

"You promised Chris what?" Kyle chuckled. "Miss Urban McDoodle – the girl who doesn't want to see a fly, a spider, or a mosquito, let alone sleep in an uncomfortable bed."

"This is different. I promised, and besides, I get paid for babysitting. Peter Bianco wants to go to the closing celebration at the mall. There's dancing until after midnight. The mall's going to be open all night."

"I guess I could sleep over."

Polly held up the black ski hat. "Could Peter Bianco be one of the Random Vandals?"

Kyle shook his head, "Doesn't seem the type, somehow. He may be a messy housekeeper and an absentminded dad, but he's not mean." Kyle sat at the dining room table putting puzzle pieces into a bag. "Nothing fits, does it?"

"What do you mean?" Polly tossed the dishrag in the sink and dropped into the chair beside him.

"This case is more chaotic than this apartment. We've got the smashed bus shelter, the smashed mural, and the smashed old car. Second, we have painted magpies appearing everywhere."

Polly picked up two pieces of the puzzle near her elbow. "We just have to be patient and try every combination."

"No one piece is going to hold all the others together," Kyle said.

"You're thinking there are two things going on here," Polly said.

"Two at least — the magpie or Graffiti Ghost as you call him, and the Random Vandals." Kyle placed the plastic bag with all the puzzle pieces in the box and fastened the ends with big chunks of cellotape.

"Neat freak."

"Dipstick," Kyle retorted.

"Computer nerd."

"Artsy-fartsy," Kyle blushed.

"Watch your language, mean bean." Polly moved toward the door. "We better find Chris and George." She tucked the cellphone in her shorts pocket.

"I bet he's in the tree fort. He may have hauled the dog up there."

Sure enough, when they got outside, there was the dog looking down on them from the fort, barking joyfully. George wagged his tail, happy as an astronaut on his first flight to the moon.

"Pass that dog down, Chris," Polly hollered. "Before he falls and breaks a leg. I'm tempted to give you a list of rules – but you keep doing more dumb things."

"Kids do dumb things," Kyle said. "It's inevitable."

"Okay, wisemouth," Polly laughed.

Kyle climbed halfway up the ladder.

Chris awkwardly handed the terrier down to Kyle. George nearly broke away and ran into the lane. Polly grabbed him by the collar and tied him to a post that held the plugs for car heaters in the winter. Drawn on it was a small magpie the size of a quarter. The Graffiti Ghost must live close by. She looked up and down the lane. The back gate to Mr. Payne's house swung wide. There was a small plastic bag of garbage by his fence. How did that get there?

"Can I bring my sleeping bag up here now? Can I?" Chris clambered down the rope ladder. "This is the best place in the whole world. I want to live here forever. I'll never leave. I can be anything I want in this tree fort – a pirate, an astronaut, a ship's captain, you name it."

"We should have a snack and go over and see this new café." Polly unwrapped George's leash from the post and led him and Chris across the parking lot to the back door of the building. She closed the door after them. Then she rejoined Kyle in the parking lot at the base of the old tree fort. The smell of leaves and twigs reminded Polly of how good she felt about herself and about the world around her. "I want to see Peter's work, don't you?"

"Just where is this gallery?" Kyle asked.

"It's that skinny store across from the Wizard's Lair. There's a magpie on the window – on brown paper – inside the locked front window."

"Aha, the plot thickens." Kyle whistled through his

teeth. "The Graffiti Ghost must be one of the boys."

"Or someone with master keys to the mall stores," Polly said. "Like Harold."

"Mike must work late at the movie theatre," Kyle said. "I wonder about him."

"Peter Bianco has keys to the art supply store," Polly said. "I've seen him lock up."

"Right."

"Could someone be using Michael Payne's name?" asked Polly. "Hanging around his house?" She thought of the small garbage bag by the back fence.

"What did you say Mike the movie usher's last name was?" Kyle asked again.

The blue-haired boy with the narrow head, big nose and big ears, thought Polly. "Mike, that's all he calls himself." She needed to stare at her sketchbook, look at her drawings of the kids in the mall. "Mike who?" Why does he look familiar?

Wind whipped across the empty back lot. Leaves, papers, even grass clippings and sand, blew fiercely. The back door of the apartment building was hard to open, pressure from the cool gusts keeping it closed. Polly knew she'd have to go in and make a sandwich for Chris.

"Are you sure we should have a sleepout?" Kyle asked.

"I'm not afraid of a little rain," Chris shouted from Polly's balcony. George woofed, his hairy muzzle sticking out through the iron railing. "We can put a tarp over us."

"A tarp won't help in a thunderstorm."

"It will pass. Won't it?" Chris said hopefully.

The two detectives went inside. Polly put George

back in Isabel's apartment, gave him fresh water and a dog biscuit. She made Chris a peanut butter and jelly sandwich. He raced up to his apartment and came down the stairs dragging his Star Trek sleeping bag, Mickey Mouse pillow, and a stuffed panda wearing a lifejacket.

"I'll get my suitcase later." He headed out the door to the tree fort, whistling TV commercials all the way.

"We're just sleeping out one night, Chris. Relax." Polly shook her head.

AFTER LUNCH in the tree fort of sandwiches, apple juice, and Rice Krispie squares that were a little over the hill, Polly, Kyle, and Chris headed over to the mall. The place was packed. Storm clouds hung in the grey sky. Gusts of wind blew scraps of paper, old leaflets, and loose gravel across the parking lot. The huge tents strained at their ropes. The canvas flapped in the wind; flags snapped and furled. Polly, the Insignificant and Insecure, worried about their plans.

"Being in the mall this afternoon will be safer than outside," she said, as they threaded their way through the crowds. Chris asked permission to hurry over to his dad's store and go with him to the launch of the mural. Polly said he could go, but he had to promise to go straight to his father. He ran off, dipping and diving through the crowd.

Gladys and Harold were having a coffee break at the Second Cup. They waved.

Polly and Kyle walked over to them. "This is my friend, Kyle Clay," Polly said. "He's been away at computer camp. Now that he's back our private investigation can accelerate." Kyle covered his mouth with his hand. Polly figured he was laughing at her using big words like him.

"We've been working on the mysteries in the mall," Kyle said quietly.

"Pleased to meet you," Harold said. "So you're Polly's friend."

"It's nice to meet some good kids. Isn't it, Harold?" Gladys patted Harold's hand. "He gets some upset by those mall rats."

"Hooligans. That's what they are," Harold said.

His face looks pale like old paste wax, thought Polly. I don't think he's a very healthy guy. "Aren't you feeling well, Mr. Palmer?"

Harold stirred his nearly empty cup of coffee with a skinny brown plastic stick. "I want to apologize for accusing you of being a thief, Polly. You were innocent." He looked up briefly, then away. "I have made some major mistakes lately."

"He keeps talking about Isabel and the mural and how sorry he was about the vandalism," Gladys said. "Harold would have stopped it if he could have, you know." She pulled her chair close to Harold, as if she were his bodyguard. Her pink track suit whispered as she moved.

"Tell Isabel, Harold." Polly grinned at the old couple. "She knows you did the best you could."

Harold shuffled his feet and looked away. "Those mall rats in black hats. I've heard them swearing and cursing. They are angry kids. I was angry too."

"It's because your wife, Mabel, died, you know." Gladys put their cups back on the tray. She walked toward the garbage disposal.

"I need to move on, that's what Isabel said." Harold pulled a tidy white hanky out of his shirt pocket and wiped his forehead.

"She's right," Polly said. She and Kyle both nodded. Polly gulped and added, "There are more good kids than bad, Mr. Palmer. Just give them a chance."

"Call me Harold, Polly." The old man blinked. It looked to Polly like he was crying.

WHEN POLLY AND KYLE reached the area by the art and framing shop where Peter worked, they found quite a busy scene. Peter had a crowd around him as he made caricatures. Chris was sitting near the front, waving furiously. He had saved seats for Polly and Kyle.

Nearby, the winner of a new red Miata, the raffle prize that had been on display all week, was sitting in the driver's seat. A beautiful blonde woman was handing him the keys, and television cameras rolled from A Channel and CTV. Two policemen walked by in uniform, complete with guns in holsters. Mike, dressed as a theatre usher, came running over. "Hurry," he said to Polly, Kyle, and Chris. "It's the unveiling of the mural in ten minutes. Then you have to go and see the Starving Artists Gallery/Café. We've told Peter to be at the end of the hall – that someone wants to meet him, someone who wants him to draw a special caricature."

"Where are Maeve and the boys?" Chris asked. "Is she still mad at Daddy?"

"Maeve is at the gallery/café," Mike hesitated. "I don't know how mad she is. What happened between them?"

Chris shrugged. "Are you coming? Where are the other boys?"

"I have to work the matinee in an hour." Mike tugged on one large ear, the one with the gold earring. "Bruce and Josh, who knows? They've been acting funny lately. Sometimes they're right with you, sometimes they disappear."

"Both Maeve and the twins hang out with the Dragonflies some, I think," Polly said.

"Not me," said Mike. "They have a real bad attitude."

"The twins play games with them at the Wizard's Lair," said Polly. "What about Josh and Bruce?"

"Culprits or just conflicted?" asked Kyle.

Chris hung his head. "I thought they liked me. I made Josh a pipe cleaner man." Crowds swirled around. Kids carried balloon animals or candy; two men with strollers tried to make it to the main doors. Rain slashed against the windows. People from the beer tent and the outdoor stage huddled in the food fair or wandered the crowded hallways. The air smelled of candy floss and coffee.

"Let's head over to the mural, Polly." Kyle took Chris's hand and dived through the mob. Polly pushed her way through like a dolphin swimming against a current.

As she swirled past Peter, she waved. "I've got Chris with me – and your phone is dead."

Peter's hand went to his head. "Oh-oh," he said. "I think I forgot to pay the bill."

The mall construction folk had put together a sturdy aluminum and wood stage with steps right in front of the mural. A red skirt went all around it. The mayor, the city councillors for the ward, Isabel, and the judges from the competition sat in a row. A small group of metal chairs was arranged close to the mural. A gold curtain hung across the whole scene.

Polly couldn't help it. She had knots in her stomach, thinking of all the work that Isabel had done, and the excitement of having helped her, even if it was a teeny bit. Harold Palmer stood at the side of the stage. His head was bowed so low it was a wonder he could see anything but his shoes. This time he didn't have any dandruff, so Polly wasn't tempted to go wipe it off. Gladys sat in the back row, knitting.

Why did adult ceremonies take so long to get going? One chair was empty. Who were they waiting for? Polly tapped her foot impatiently. Chris crawled under the skirts of the stage after a jawbreaker he'd gotten from the gum machine. Polly hauled him out and plunked him on the seat beside her. Then she took out her sketchbook, flipped back a few pages, checking something. She leaned close to Kyle.

"Does Harold have dandruff or doesn't he? And how fast can you get rid of it?"

Kyle stared at her over the top of his glasses and then sidled over to Harold and asked him a question. Harold raised his head for a moment and then bent forward again.

Kyle hurried back to where Polly was standing. "I saw no trace of dandruff anywhere. His hair looks greasy like he uses some kind of gel in it. Why?" Kyle asked.

"I've got a funny feeling about this, that's all."

The last person had finally arrived and taken her chair.

"If Harold doesn't have dandruff, what were all the

flecks on his left shoulder last week?" Polly pointed to the sketch in her book with the date on it. Harold standing behind Gladys in a clean black guard shirt with flecks all over it.

"Right at that moment, Isabel was discovering that her mural had been smashed." Polly squinted. "I can't believe it. Is Harold the Random Vandal?"

"Or the jealous loser?" asked Kyle.

The two of them stared at each other for a moment.

"Perhaps he saw someone hitting the mural and didn't stop them," Polly said.

"That would explain the guilt," Kyle said. "He said he'd made some big mistakes lately."

The lady beside them put her finger to her lips. The two detectives stopped talking.

Speeches were made. Applause resounded. Out of the corner of her eye, Polly watched as Mike, the theatre usher, joined the crowd grouped by the mural. He stood on the far side, close to the emergency exit. "What kind of artwork does Mike do?" Polly mused. "Have we ever seen any of it? What's his full name?"

Kyle moved over to the teenager, asked him a question. Mike took change out of his pocket and they traded pieces of money.

In a moment, Kyle was back beside Polly. "He's got smudged, artists' fingers, just like you. I got a good look at his hands to check that out by asking for change. He gave me change for a five-dollar bill. Says his last name is Smith. He said he did cartooning best, but he likes doing real stuff too."

"Right. I'm not convinced about the name. It could be an alias."

"What do we know about him?" Kyle whispered. He looked like he wanted to say more but hesitated. "We see a lot of him, don't we?"

"His folks don't want him to be an artist. He's come here to stay with his uncle, but can't find him at home and no one answers his phone. That's what he told me."

"So where is he staying?" Kyle stared at Mike and munched sunflowers from his pocket.

"I think it is near our place."

Kyle nodded in agreement.

"He keeps appearing in our back lane." Polly frowned, flipped to her sketch of Mike. "He has very big ears – just like one of the men in Isabel's mural. And why is he so interested in this mural? It's as if he felt some personal stake in it." Polly put her finger to her lips. The mayor and Isabel were moving to the curtain. A TV cameraman shouldered through the crowd beside Polly. The reporter with him was talking –

"When we finish here, there's a story at a small coffee shop/gallery. It's opening day and they're displaying a local artist. Should get two good minutes from this whole show."

All Isabel's work, all Peter Bianco's work, was worth a total of two minutes? It didn't seem fair to Polly. Wasn't art worth more than that?

The mayor reached for the curtain pull. Everyone poised to clap. There was a sudden silence. The curtain caught and finally, swish – the mural was revealed. In the background someone put on a CD of one of Edmonton's brass ensembles playing a fanfare.

"A tribute to our fair city's history and our fine artists," the mayor spoke into the television mike. The chipper reporter in her bright red suit, her makeup impeccable, her hair gleaming, stood grinning beside him. The crowd clapped. Isabel blushed and Harold tied the curtains back with gold silk ropes. Polly found the whole scene a little much. "Looks like the important people are the mayor and the TV reporter, not the historical people in the mural, and the artist."

"Don't tell me you're getting cynical, Polly?" Kyle smiled a slow smile. "What ever happened to the Innocent Polly McDoodle?"

"This should be Isabel's day. That's all."

"Thousands of people will walk past this mural in the next few years. They will see it, not television cameras and officials." Kyle bent and tied up his sneaker. "This is Isabel's day. Let's go tell her."

Two things happened in the next minute that shed a new light on everything – young Mike walked really close to the end of the mural, bent over, and touched the painted magpie, and Harold keeled over. Gladys ran to Harold. Polly's eyes took it all in. She looked from Mike's long narrow smiling face with its skinny nose, big ears, and shocking blue hair. Then she glanced over where Harold lay on the marble floor, a man who looked like a doctor bending over him. Soon, a couple of ambulance attendants arrived with a stretcher and Harold was wheeled out the door. Gladys trotted behind, her shoulders hunched, her head bowed. The siren sounded loud as it hurried away. The television cameraman and the reporter hurried after them.

"At least the hospital is really close." Isabel held out her hand as if searching for a cane or some support. Mike Smith reached her before Polly and Kyle.

"You look awfully familiar, young man," Isabel said, as he sat beside her on one of the low benches near the mural. "Mike's nephew, I gather. I knew Mike Payne when he was your age. He wore a ponytail in those days. A pipefitter with a hippie heart."

"You're Michael Payne's nephew?" Polly asked, holding the sketch of him up to the light. The resemblance was unmistakable, blue hair notwithstanding.

"I wonder if you've been sleeping on your uncle's back porch?" Kyle mumbled. "Wouldn't have borrowed a sleeping bag, would you?" Polly remembered telling Kyle about the missing sleeping bag.

"I didn't think Isabel would need it." Mike blushed.

"It wasn't Isabel's, goofus, it was ours," Polly said. "My mom gave me grief over that."

"Sorry," Mike blushed again. "I'll bring it back."

Polly paused, stared thoughtfully at Mike, then flipped through her sketchbook to the front. "You wouldn't like to give me some pointers on drawing these, would you?" She held up her early picture of magpies, nest and all.

Mike whispered, "You draw them too?"

"Not on doors, windows, bus shelters, and who knows where else," Polly said.

"They're cheeky birds who let you know they're around by squawking," Mike said. "I want people to know I'm around – so I draw."

"Believe me, we all know now. You're the Graffiti Ghost, aren't you? That's the nickname we gave you."

Mike nodded. "MP – Magpie or Mike Payne."

"What about Smith?" Polly asked.

"That's my mother's name."

"So, will you give me some pointers? Your magpies are really great."

"Thanks."

Isabel patted Mike's arm. "You will have a mural of your own one day. Meanwhile the painted magpies remind us all."

"I think I had better confine my talents to paper from now on, don't you?" Mike grinned.

Just then a couple of well-wishers came to talk to Isabel. Polly, Chris, and Kyle left. The kid had been surprisingly quiet during the whole opening.

"I'm hungry," said Chris. "Are you hungry?"

"How did you figure out that Mike was sleeping at Mr. Payne's?" Polly asked Kyle as they went in search of ice cream.

"Elementary, my dear Polly," Kyle laughed, as he tried to imitate Sherlock Holmes talking to Watson. "I didn't want to say anything until I was sure. When my parents and I drove in from Small Shadow Lake he was letting himself out of Payne's garden gate. He ducked down the lane in the opposite direction. He couldn't see us sitting in the car."

"You never told me. That's not fair." Polly punched Kyle's arm.

"I didn't figure out the significance right away."

"You didn't know who he was?" Polly asked.

"Not until you filled me in on all the events, people, and clues later," Kyle grinned.

"I'm glad you're home, Kyle." Polly heaved a sigh. "I don't know why I didn't see him, though."

"You've been pretty busy."

Polly nodded. "Two heads are better than one. I'm

glad we're a detective team." She grinned at Kyle. "I hope Harold's going to be all right. He may be grumpy but he's part of the mall."

Chris took ages choosing his double scoop cone when they got to the ice cream store. "Let's go see Daddy."

The three walked to the gallery/café. Peter was talking to everyone at once. He smiled, shook hands, and waved toward his gathered paintings. Chris tagged along with him, licking his ice cream, grinning like the cat that had swallowed the cream.

"How do you like the show, Polly?" Peter asked. "It's a surprise. Imagine that kid of mine not spilling the beans. Too bad Maeve is so mad at me. She says she's angry and knows some other angry people she'd rather hang out with, people who take things into their own hands. I'm happy. I wish she could be happy too."

He had done several large canvasses with what looked like old-fashioned paintings on wrinkled brown cloth. There was a group of sketches of young Chris. The guy could draw. He obviously loved his little boy. Polly bit her lip. How did you separate a person's life from their art? "I'm impressed." That was all she could say.

"Me too," said Kyle.

They waved goodbye to Chris, promising to meet him later.

"MALLS ARE FUNNY PLACES," KYLE reflected as they walked back to the mural. They had stopped to visit Polly's dad in his sports store, but Ted was busy selling a pair of basketball shoes to a guy who towered over him a good foot and a half.

"Filled with giants and kids," Polly said. She really wanted to draw that tall basketball player with the long arms and neck. If he'd had spotted skin and pointy ears, he could have passed for a giraffe.

"No, a mall is a cross between a town in a bubble and a mechanical toy," Kyle said. "It's lights, music, action, but no story."

"My, we are waxing serious," Polly said as they turned the corner into the corridor leading to the Seniors' Centre and the mural. Ahead of them, a jeweller and a potter were picking up their table and chairs, broken pots, and capsized displays. Officer Connelly stood nearby.

"What happened?" Polly asked.

"A group of teens came running down the hall, chasing each other," the potter said. "Two of them ran right into the table, knocking our whole display down. The ones coming behind joined in the 'fun.'"

"Did you recognize any of them?" Kyle asked.

"They all look the same to me – dressed in black, baggy pants and dangling earrings. One needed a shave. They smelled bad. Three of them wore black ski hats pulled down to cover their foreheads." The pottery artist's hands shook, her voice was shrill as she gathered her precious work or what was left of it.

Polly bent, helping the women put things back together. She grabbed a broom and swept up the shards of broken pots. "Thank goodness, they didn't touch the main display of pottery."

On the floor beside a piece of a blue kiln-glazed

teapot lay an earring – a dragonfly with silver wings. Polly picked it up carefully. She glanced at both the potter and the jeweller. Both of them had dangling summer earrings.

"Is this one of yours?" Polly asked the jeweller.

"No, I don't make them with that design."

"Can I take it then?" Polly asked. "I might know whose it is." She wrapped the earring in a tissue and placed it carefully in her jean pocket. She also picked up several small items strewn across the floor.

"May I ask you a question?" Polly asked the jeweller. "Do you display other people's work as well as your own?"

"I stick to selling my own stuff," the woman said. "I've been asked to show others. But I don't want to be responsible for it. We're out here in a corridor."

"Do you remember who asked you in the last week?" Polly leaned close to the jeweller. She had a very soft voice and the mall was noisy.

She shook her head. "I didn't pay much attention. My standard answer is no. One young person shouted at me, as if it was my fault she didn't have the money to rent a booth."

"I'd really like you to think about this," Polly said. "I'm trying to help the police solve the problem they are having with vandalism in the mall."

"Pretty young to be a detective, aren't you?" the woman chuckled. "If I think of anything I'll let you know. I've seen you before. Your dad runs the sports store doesn't he? Ted McDougall?"

Polly nodded.

"She was short and skinny. Wore black, that kid that

shouted at you did," the potter added. "But then again, they all do."

"Thanks," Polly said.

By the time she and Kyle got back to the mural, Isabel had gone.

"Isabel and that young man Mike went to the hospital to check on his uncle and Harold," the volunteer coordinator told them. Mr. Russell grinned as if nothing could ever faze him. "This week Murphy's Law has been in full flood. Whatever can go wrong, will go wrong. What with magpies and vandals, and incidents and accidents, and storms threatening."

"Things are finally improving." Polly smiled at Mr. Russell. "We've found our Graffiti Ghost. His name is Mike Payne, the younger."

"Does Isabel know everyone in the province, or what?" Kyle laughed. The two of them headed out the doors and home for a break.

"Tonight's the big sleepout," Polly said. "And Erin should be back. Let's get moving."

WHEN THEY GOT HOME, they discovered Polly's parents loading their car for the trip. Everything was labeled and piled neatly.

"Oh, it's such a relief to see you Polly," her mother sighed. "Are you sure you shouldn't come with us? I tried phoning Rachel, but she's out."

Polly's dad stood behind his wife, shrugging his shoulders and grinning at Polly. "Polly's a big girl. She'll be fine. She's staying with Erin."

"There might be a storm."

"We won't stay outside if there's a storm, Mom." Polly gave her mom and dad hugs and nudged them toward the car. "You don't want to be late for the wedding."

"You've got our cellphone in your pocket and the hotel number in Red Deer if you need us. The reception is in the hotel ballroom. They'll page us if you call." Her mother hung her head out the car window.

"Mom, I'll be fine."

Finally Polly's parents drove off.

"Your folks," Kyle laughed. "They'll probably go on your first date with you."

Polly watched the exhaust from her parent's car rise in the back lane. For some reason, she felt warmed. Maybe Ted and Jan McDougall were overprotective, but it made Polly feel really safe, no matter what the night ahead might bring.

10. Three Heads are Better

"SO TELL ME ALL ABOUT IT." ERIN STRETCHED HER long legs across the ratty floor of the tree house. It was evening and the four kids had gathered in the tree fort. "I need a full report." Her straight black hair hung down, partially covering her smooth cinnamon-coloured face with its dark eyes, long lashes, and broad forehead. She folded her hands like a tent and listened intently.

"It all started..." Chris hopped up on the side railing, "when Dad and I moved into the apartment."

"When I was accused by Harold of spilling paint and stealing stuff," Polly said. "I should phone Isabel and find out how he's doing."

"It started when I got a panic call from Polly," said Kyle bluntly, "That's when I knew we had a Random Vandal and Graffiti Ghost."

"This is my story. Let me tell it." Chris leaped down from his perch on the railing. "I want to tell." He danced around the wooden tree fort like a raccoon on skates, all dart and dash. The fort could hardly hold the four of them. It was going to be a tight fit for the sleepover.

Kyle sat up on the railing, Erin pulled her knees to her chin, and Polly curled in the corner. Chris tipped over Polly's red milk crate, dumping out her markers and her latest sketchbook. "There'll be a record in here."

"Cool your jets, Chris!" Polly tried to grab her book back.

"I've been wanting to see this." Chris danced away, pulled himself up on the railing, and opened the sketch-book. He flipped through the pages.

"Here's a picture of me up in this tree fort – I look better than that. There's some words written under-neath. 'Rules for growing up, Number One: *Respect the space of others.*'"

"Let me have that," Polly demanded.

"Here's another one of me. It says 'Number Two: *Don't take things that don't belong to you.*' There's a sketch of me tossing elastic bands."

"Chris, that's my book. You shouldn't be looking at it."

"'Rule Number Three: *Don't talk all the time.*' It's me with my mouth open and a magpie screaming from a tree branch." Chris looked over at Polly, her hand still reaching out for her sketches. "I don't like this book."

Kyle and Erin said nothing. They both looked uncomfortable. Polly grabbed at the book and wrestled with Chris until she freed it from his grip. "That's private."

"You made fun of me!" Chris shouted. "I thought you were my friend."

"I am your friend."

"Friends don't tease."

"I'm not teasing. You've got a lot to learn."

"So have you! Yes, you do!" Chris cried. "You aren't a nice person."

"I am so," Polly blustered. "I just wanted to help."

"How many rules you got for me, Polly?" Chris crouched in the corner with his Star Trek sleeping bag wrapped around him. "Hundreds? Thousands?"

"Polly was trying to help," Erin said softly.

"You are a little wild," Kyle added. But he was looking at Polly with a hint of disappointment in his eyes. "Good reader, though, for a little kid."

Chris shrugged when he heard that.

"I don't want to fight," Polly said. "Let's change the subject."

"Maybe I should go away," Chris sighed. "You don't like me, you just put up with me. Don't you?"

"We like you," Polly sighed. "Let's forget it, okay."

The kid stood in the middle of the fort regarding them suspiciously. He was pouting and his face was red.

"A change of scenery, perhaps," suggested Erin. "You could go for snacks, Chris. Check on your dad. Let us talk to Polly for a minute."

"Talk about manners." Kyle chewed his bottom lip.

"Go get some junk food for us. There's some in my apartment on the counter," Polly said. "You are the gofer aren't you?" Her ears were pounding and her face felt hot. Chris shouldn't have tipped over her crate and taken her sketchbook. A storm brewed in her head. She had wanted to choose the time to give him the rules.

"I need cheese treats," Erin moaned, "to feed my starved brain."

"Cookies or bananas for me," Kyle said. "I think better with fruit."

"Things go better with fruit," Erin giggled. "Juice would be good." The two of them were obviously trying to make things better, to calm Polly and Chris down. Maybe the kid would lighten up. Polly hoped so.

It was so good to have her buddies back. They'd help her figure things out. She'd rely on them. She smiled encouragingly and gave Chris a key to her apartment. "My mom left all those goodies in our kitchen."

He took the key, glared at her, and disappeared down the ladder. "Don't touch my sleeping bag."

"Take your time, short one," Erin sang out.

"McDoodle and Clay...." Kyle announced.

"And Associates," added Erin.

"Have business to discuss," said Kyle.

Chris sighed long and loud and stomped across the parking lot toward the back door. "You've been mean, Polly. I don't like you any more," he yelled back at Polly.

"Chris is a cute kid," Polly said, "but he gets on my nerves. He needs a lot of attention and talks too much."

"Typical kid, eh?" Kyle munched a handful of sunflower seeds.

"If you're going to write rules under your pictures, you should keep them hidden," Erin said.

"I wasn't expecting him to grab my sketchbook."

"Haven't you said anything nice about the kid?" Kyle asked.

"I did."

"When?" Kyle's voice was hard-edged.

Polly hung her head. "In Rule Number Ten I was nice...."

"Number Ten, eh?" Erin said.

"Rule Number Ten is *Remember what a great kid you*

are at all times." Polly said. "I wrote that the other day when I figured out he was missing his mom so much." She held up the latest page. "I even put them all on one page so I could make him a copy."

"You should tell him the last rule for sure," Kyle said. "A kid needs to have positive reinforcement."

Polly nodded. "I will, when he gets back with the munchies."

"Back to the case." Erin sounded businesslike and super mature.

Polly shrugged. Her friends, she sighed. Kyle, the logical and sometimes humorous geek and Erin, the tough, intelligent but often smartass teen queen. Meanwhile, there she was, the Dishevelled, Disorganized McDoodle, insensitive babysitter, arts freak, and amateur detective.

Kyle took out a notebook. Polly pulled a different sketchbook out of her backpack. She put the offending one back in her milk crate. Erin began braiding fine bright-coloured plastic strips together to make a bracelet.

"What are the crimes? Who are the suspects? Do we have any clues or witnesses?" Erin asked.

"Slow down," Kyle demanded.

They went through the whole story piece by piece, studied Polly's pictures, listed the potential suspects, their possible motives, and clues.

"First, there were paints and brushes taken from the back of the art supply store," Polly said. "Harold accused me of that."

"Then there was the smashed bus shelter and the vandalized car. Right, Polly?" Kyle asked.

"About the same time as Isabel's mural was hammered," Polly said. "That crime drew my attention. Kyle suggested I find out who had submitted entries for the mural. Someone also broke into the mall office and trashed everything."

"So the prime suspects are Harold, Mike, Peter Bianco, and Josh and Bruce," Erin summed up. "Harold is jealous of Isabel. Mike is feeling isolated and abandoned. Peter could be jealous of Isabel or just angry at not being chosen. Josh and Bruce might be jealous, but we don't know if they had entered the mural competition."

"What about Maeve?" Kyle asked.

"She wasn't one of the artists. She does jewellery."

"But she does hang out with the Dragonflies, not just Peter's gang," Kyle reflected.

"So do Josh and Bruce," added Polly.

"One of the rejected artists might have smashed the mural," said Erin.

"That doesn't explain the other acts of vandalism," Kyle said. "That only works for the mural. Didn't Officer Connelly say that often vandalism is random, done by a small group who are just angry or want to be noticed?"

"He talked about perpetrators. I don't see Harold as a perpetrator," Polly said. "He's too busy marching around in his uniform, giving kids a hard time."

"He had a hammer and plenty of opportunity," Erin commented.

"So did Peter Bianco. Didn't you say Chris had his dad's hammer when he was putting his sign on our fort?" Kyle said. "We know he also has a black ski hat.

Polly found it when she was cleaning their apartment."

"Mall rats in black hats," Erin chuckled.

"There was one in the back of his van too, but that could have been left there by anyone – Mike, Josh and Bruce, or Maeve." Polly sighed and shook her head. "We don't know enough about Josh and Bruce, or it could be someone entirely different."

"You've got that earring you found," Erin said.

"See if anyone is missing one." Polly flipped through her sketchbook. "We all need to be paying attention to details."

"Right." Kyle saluted.

"Are you supposed to be keeping an eye on Chris?" Erin asked after she had agreed to the plan.

"No, his dad said he'd be around after supper."

"Where's our snacks?" asked Kyle, the ravenous.

"I'll run in and check on him." Polly clambered down the rope ladder. "I can tell him Rule Number Ten and apologize again."

Inside, she found her apartment door open and the key on the counter beside the snack food. There was no sign of Chris. She ran up the stairs to Chris's apartment and knocked loudly. Peter Bianco opened the door, rubbing sleep from his eyes.

"Have you seen Chris?" Polly asked.

"Sure, he was here a little while ago," he murmured. "Chris, where are you?" There was no answer in the cluttered apartment. Polly could see a stack of canvasses in the hallway and an easel propped up in the corner of the living room with a new painting half finished. The air smelled of dust bunnies and acrylic paints. But it was homey, too, in a true Bianco style – not a

McDougall style – but a Bianco. Polly's ears felt itchy as if she was learning something, hearing something inside. One of her dad's sayings, "Don't judge others." She had been busy judging Peter and Chris, hadn't she? Her mouth felt dry.

"That's funny. I was sure he was here," Peter said. "I came home for a sleep. I was up most of last night helping set up the closing celebration. Then those young people surprised me with my one-person show in that new little gallery/café. It was too exciting for words. What did you think of it? Did you like my work? There were TV cameras. I even sold a painting. I got exhausted. Came home. Thought I'd catch a few winks before I go back. Told the kid to take care of himself for awhile. Tonight's going to be a real blast. Are you coming?"

Polly shut her eyes and opened them again. "Volunteers are having their celebration next week. I'll wait until then." Then she paused. "Do you want me to go over to the mall and check on him?" She thought of her friends, sleeping bags and all, up in the old tree fort. They had so much to discuss. But she needed to smooth Chris's ruffled feathers. Watch it, Polly, the kid is not a bird. He's a lonely mixed-up little person.

"I'll go. It's time I went and joined in the fun," Peter shook himself like a dozy dog. "Did I tell you everything about the new gallery and café? Television cameras came by. Imagine those kids deciding to mount my work. They talked the guy into it. I'm really good, but no one knows it, because I don't get the exposure I need. I...."

Polly stood for a couple of more seconds in the doorway, listening as he talked about himself and his work.

Didn't he worry about his kid? "So you'll check on Chris? He was planning on sleeping out in the tree fort with us tonight." Polly just hoped that her drawings and rules hadn't discouraged him too much. "Call me on my parents' cellphone if there's a problem." She made sure he had the number written down in his Daytimer.

"Good. I can party the night away then." Peter nodded and shut the door. Loud rock music soon blared from behind Bianco's door as Polly headed back down the stairs. She stopped by her apartment to pick up the snacks, raid the cupboard, and the refrigerator. There were more goodies than usual, because her brother was off at camp. Her stomach growled in anticipation. "Shut up, stomach," the Famished McDoodle said.

THE THREE KIDS demolished the snacks. Kyle got Brutus from his apartment and Polly collected George. They walked the two dogs to the pocket park and let them run around. The dogs explored a collection of metal objects piled on a gravel pad. Some hubcaps, wheel rims, fenders and a shopping trolley were half-bolted together. Brutus pawed at a ketchup packet and George sniffed a dropped french fries container.

"Is that a half-finished sculpture or a miniature auto wreckers'?" Kyle asked.

"It's weird," Erin said. "If it's a sculpture, the artist doesn't have a very high opinion of our society."

"Like Polly's mall rats," said Kyle.

Polly just glanced at the work in progress and shook her head. She had more important things to think about. "I don't like this mystery. It's all inside the mall.

There's no environmental angle."

"Environment is everywhere," said Erin. "A mall is a commercial environment, climate-controlled, enclosed, relatively safe and secure, well-lit, geared to shoppers and strollers, buyers and sellers. You can snack or dine, listen to mall music, or watch wide-screen television in a store window."

"You can choose pets in the pet store, watch your child play in the daycare centre, play bingo, or have your hair done," Kyle added. "You can hang out, meander all day, or just dash in and purchase what you need."

"What's with you two?" Polly asked. "I'm trying to get a hold of the crime, not write an essay on the whole philosophy of malls."

"Think about it, Polly," Erin said. "What if someone thought a mall was the most important place in their life? What would that do to them?"

"Mall addicts?" Kyle quipped. "Reduce life to what you need, want, and desire. Greed, possessions, and canned entertainment."

"I think your Random Vandal is sick – maybe with mall fever, envy, or an evil temper," Erin stated. "A smash-and-burn attitude."

Polly shook her head. Trust her friends to put a twist on what had looked like a simple crime. Now she'd have to think the whole thing through again. They took the dogs back to their apartments. Both of them were woofing at the wind in the trees all the way back. "It's only the wind," said Kyle. "Don't get spooked."

"Do you think we should wait for Chris?" Polly asked. Peter waved at them as he left for the mall with a painting wrapped in a tarp.

"What about Chris?" Polly hollered after him.

"He'll be at the mall, Polly. Don't worry, I'll look for him." The back lane acted like a wind tunnel whipping Peter's jacket tight against his slim body, blowing stray papers in front of him as he walked to the corner. "He'll probably be back soon."

"Funny, isn't it? Chris was the one who wanted to sleep outdoors in the fort so badly," Kyle said. "Now he's disappeared."

Polly hoped she hadn't hurt the kid's feelings too much. "Kids bounce back fast, don't they?" She laughed, thinking that she was beginning to talk like Chris, putting a question at the end of every sentence.

Kyle ordered a pizza on Polly's cellphone, with money his folks had left him. He told them to tell the delivery guy to bring it to the tree fort.

The sky was overcast, with clouds rolling swiftly across the grey horizon. It was getting dark by the time the three of them arranged their sleeping bags in the fort, curled up, and talked. Polly left the cellphone turned on and propped up on her milk crate. They tidied Chris's corner and arranged his sleeping bag and backpack as well. Chris didn't show up. They ate the pizza when it came and left two pieces for Chris.

The old willow tree rocking in the rising wind lulled them to sleep. Erin had a new Walkman that her Uncle Eustace Cardinal had given her while she had been visiting the northern Cree band. Polly had asked her to turn on the weather report before they dozed off, but Erin forgot. They fell asleep chatting about the mysteries at the mall. Polly worried briefly about Chris. Then she comforted herself that Chris was his father's responsibility. They were probably together.

POLLY DREAMED of being in a cable car suspended over a chasm. Wind and rain surrounded her. She was swaying in a metal box. Beneath her was air and more air and, far below, a carpeted tropical forest floor. The drop would kill her. She gasped in fear. The cables whined, groaned, and snapped, and she was flung out into space. She tried to fly, but couldn't. She tried to scream, but no sounds came out of her mouth. Her ears pounded as she plummeted to the ground. She struggled to wake up, to get away from the dream.

"Polly, wake up!" Was Kyle shaking her? No he wasn't, the whole tree was shaking, quivering like the cable car in her dreams. It was dark. Rain pounded the leaves. The wooden floor of the fort was soaked. Sirens wailed nearby. Darkness, torrential rain, and wind beat at the tree fort and its three inhabitants. The floodlight for the parking lot flickered. It could not compete with the rain, wind, and darkness.

Polly, Kyle, and Erin tumbled over each other, yanked at sodden sleeping bags, slipped on the soaked ladder rungs, and ran through the deluge to the back entrance. They clustered in the vestibule, searching for a key.

"Mom and Constable Joe Haynes are at a movie," Erin gasped for breath as she talked.

"My parents are at a lecture on the law and civil liberties." Kyle shook his head like a wet dog, spraying everyone around him with raindrops. "I hope they're okay."

"Mine are safe in Red Deer." Polly's parents had gone to the wedding of the Excel Sports manager there. Polly and Erin would take care of each other.

Lightning slashed across the sky and the lights up and down the street and in the apartment building went out. Erin turned her key in the lock. The three hurried up the stairs to Polly's apartment. Polly felt around, scraping the door key around the lock until she finally got it in right. Once inside, Polly rummaged in the kitchen drawer for a flashlight. The two girls moved right to the patio doors and stared out. Polly doused the flashlight so their eyes could adjust to the dark.

"With the lights off, we can see the storm," Polly shouted. The wind rattled the windows. The sound of trees crackling, wires humming, slick tires on rain-swept streets came through the patio door. The building itself seemed to be swaying with every gust of wind. Polly's muscles tightened, her eyes burned. She did not feel very old, very mature. She wished her parents were home. Somewhere back in her history there was the story of one of the pioneer McDougalls getting lost in a storm and dying of exposure. But those were the days before apartment buildings and cars and fire departments and hospitals near by.

Kyle switched the kitchen radio onto battery power. "There is a weather advisory for Edmonton and area," the radio announcer said. "People are advised to stay indoors. Funnel-like clouds are moving through the city. A tornado is a strong possibility. Four centimetres of rain have fallen already. Winds are gusting up to one hundred and fifty miles an hour. Hail and driving rain are expected to continue into the night."

The three young people stood together staring out. Darkness surrounded them. Thunder boomed and lightning flashed. Red emergency lights shone from the top of the hospital on the Kingsway. An occasional motor vehicle swept by, its headlights revealing trees swaying like grass, loose shingles tossed like kites in the air. Otherwise, black coated everything.

The building creaked and groaned as if it was under siege. Polly shook. Her insides quivered like Jell-O. "Where's Chris? I've got to find him. He'll be scared."

She took the kitchen flashlight and made her way along the hallway and into her bedroom. Since her mom's last warning, she had kept her room fairly tidy. She didn't stumble over anything as she found her dresser. Sure enough, her flashlight was where it belonged. She flipped the switch and light flooded her room. How comforting. She left the kitchen flashlight with Kyle and Erin in the living room and let herself out the front door of the apartment.

She found her way down the hall to the stairs. The staircase creaked, the outside walls rattled like railway cars. Polly was surprised there weren't more people around. Were they cocooned in their own spaces? Where was Isabel? Still at the hospital with young Mike Payne or over at the mall?

Polly knocked on Isabel's door. George moaned and woofed. "It's all right George. Isabel will be back as soon as this storm is over. Go back and hide." Polly knew the frightened terrier liked to curl his fuzzy furry body in the front hall closet on a ratty blue blanket during storms or attacks of the deadly vacuum cleaner. His usually perky tail would be wrapped around his haunches, ears laid back, muzzle quivering. She knew how he felt. She gulped twice and made herself take a couple of deep breaths.

There was no answer at Bianco's. Polly banged and shouted just to make sure. A scary thought pushed its way to the front of her mind. What if Chris had indeed joined them in the fort? He might have slept through the whole thing. They had moved out of there so fast they hadn't even checked his corner. Polly ran down the steps as fast as she could with the aid of the flashlight. Shadows leapt and careened in the silent hall. She shuddered.

I don't know whether I should do this or not. I'm sure the "stay inside" directive was for me too. But I can't let Chris suffer. Polly's mind rolled thoughts around and around in her head like marbles in a bag. They banged each other. She took a deep breath and opened the door.

She dashed along the sidewalk, the hood of her grey sweatshirt pulled over her head as if she were a turtle in its shell. A tree branch snapped in the gale, a garbage can lid clattered and rolled down the lane. A fire truck sped down the Kingsway, lights flashing, engine clanging, and siren whining. Polly climbed quickly into the fort and peered around, shone her flashlight into all the corners. There was no sign of the boy. Chris's sleeping bag and backpack were not in the fort. At some point during the night, while she and the others had been sleeping, he must have come back and taken his belongings.

She grabbed her sketchbook, cellphone, and milk crate. No sense everything getting wet.

A clap of thunder resonated near by and a sound like crunching metal followed. The earth trembled as Polly slid off the ladder and made a beeline for the door. She used the flashlight to find the lock and let herself in. She sighed with relief. One question answered but another arose right behind it. Where could that kid have gone?

She put her art supplies by her apartment door. Drops of rain glistened on the old red milk crate.

Taking the key to Bianco's apartment she let herself in and searched through the place. No one was around. Dishes were piled in the sink as usual, clothing on the bedroom floor, a half-finished charcoal sketch of George, the dog, lay on the drawing table. The place was crammed with samples of Peter Bianco's work. Polly wished she liked Peter better. He was talented and friendly. He just didn't strike her as being a really good dad. But then had she been a good friend to Chris?

She could feel tears gathering in her eyes, sliding down her cheeks. Drawing pictures and making up rules had been so innocent, done only to help the kid. But when Chris saw those pictures, read those rules, he had been really hurt. Because of her, he might at this very moment be lost in the storm. He wasn't very smart when it came to taking care of himself.

"Polly, Polly, where are you?" Kyle's voice came from the stairwell.

"I'm coming," Polly shouted as she left Biancos' and hurried down the stairs to her own place.

Kyle grabbed her and pulled her inside. Erin carried the milk crate. He and Erin hugged her tight as soon as the door was closed.

"What's the matter with you two? Why this sudden concern?"

"We saw you go out to the tree fort."

"We missed seeing you come back in...." Erin's voice broke.

"So?"

"So, look outside."

11. Tragedy

POLLY STARED OUT THE RAIN-SPLATTERED WINDOW. Hailstones as large as golf balls struck the asphalt parking lot, bounced off car roofs, banged and cascaded down the bright red metal garage roof across the way. She shouldn't be able to see that roof. But it was plainly visible, even through the driving rain. She watched helplessly as a hunk of panelling flew across the parking lot like a tissue paper kite and smashed into a parked car, cracking the windshield into thousands of pieces.

Worst of all, the hailstones lay in piles around the smashed, buckled, and broken branches and scarred, white, shattered trunk of the old willow tree. Stark fingers of bleached trunk pierced the sky like jagged icicles or stalagmites in the dark cave of the night.

Chunks of plywood, railing, ladder, a tipped-over old trunk littered the ground. Hailstones slammed tumbled planks that littered the landscape. Their tree, their tree fort, the House of the Elusive Rabbit, lay in ruins.

The three kids stood in stony silence, their mouths

open wide, gulping air as if they were drowning in the torrent outside.

"It's gone," Polly whispered finally. She was afraid to say anything out loud. She was so glad they had wakened up in time. Her heartbeat sounded loud as thunder in her ears.

"Completely," Erin sighed.

Kyle didn't say anything. He leaned his hand on the door frame, his forehead against the patio door. "Chris?"

"He wasn't there. Neither was his sleeping bag."

"Where?" Erin asked.

"He's not in his apartment. Hopefully he's with his dad at the mall."

"In the dark?" Kyle said.

"Scary, eh?" Erin sat down on the couch. "I need to catch my breath."

Kyle nodded. "Close call."

Polly went to the kitchen and got two candles, lit them, and put them on the coffee table. The pale light danced around the walls spelling relief and safety. Their faces were glum. That tree fort was part of all of them. It was their space and it was gone.

"News is coming in from the areas of the city most affected by this storm," the announcer said. Kyle turned the radio up. "Electricity is out north of the North Saskatchewan River. Several traffic accidents have been reported as well as trees down, dented cars, roofs of houses blown off. Debris on main roads in the northeast. People are cautioned to stay off the streets. The Groat Road has several trees blocking the exit to 107th Ave. Flooding on the Yellowhead near St. Albert Trail. Storm sewers are overflowing. The underpass on 109th

Street is impassable. You are asked to keep phone lines open for emergencies."

The phone rang.

"Polly, are you all right?" her mother's voice asked anxiously.

"We're fine. Kyle and Erin are with me. The lights are out. The willow tree was struck by lightning."

"Are you sure you are all right?"

"Look, Mom, we're fine."

"Dad and I are wondering whether we should come home."

"Stay there. I'll be okay."

There was a whispered conversation on the other end.

"You won't do anything foolish, will you?"

"No."

"Promise?"

"Promise." Polly hoped she could keep it. But Chris was out there somewhere and she felt responsible. Surely the storm would pass soon. Fierce storms can't last all night, can they?

No sooner had she thought that when the lights came on, flickered a couple of times, and then stayed on.

"Hurrah!" Kyle crowed.

"I wonder where our folks are?" Erin asked. "I sure hope Mom wasn't out in that."

"Don't she and Joe usually go out for a late supper after?" Polly asked. "They talk half the night, it seems to me."

"They won't phone," Kyle added. "Constable Joe knows that the lines need to be used for emergencies."

"Maybe he went in to work," Polly suggested. "Your

mom will be fine." Polly knew how sensitive Erin was. Her dad had been killed by a drunk driver a couple of years ago. Only this last spring she had still been pretty shaky, still missing him too much. Erin didn't need to have problems with her mom too.

Polly went over to the balcony door and stared dejectedly out at the demolished tree fort. "It's a good thing we came in the house when we did."

"Where's Chris?" Kyle asked quietly. He was running his thin, bony fingers through his hair as if to dislodge an answer. "That kid worries me."

"I know what you mean," Polly said. "I'm wondering if we shouldn't go over to the mall and try to find his dad, maybe find him. The mall was staying open late because of the party." She dug in the front hall closet for rain gear and rubber boots. She slipped her parents' cell-phone into her pocket.

"I'll check my apartment. See if Mom has phoned." Erin padded across the hall and up the stairs on her bare feet. Her sandals, soggy from rain, sat by Polly's front door.

Kyle turned on the television, plopped down in the overstuffed armchair, and nibbled on sunflower seeds. Amateur video camera shots of the approaching storm, a semi-trailer jackknifed on the Yellowhead Highway, a collapsed garage, a flooded intersection, the river roiling and boiling up over its banks by more than a foot, a fly-ing rooftop, a dead cow, a huge tree twisted like a corkscrew, branches and whole trees blocking a neigh-bourhood street – all those images flashed on the screen. The reporter's voice rose above the roaring of the wind outside his studio. He was going over the list of poten-tial problem areas in the city and an up-to-date tally on injuries and accidents. Polly wanted to shut her ears and her eyes. It felt as if her heart was beating inside her eardrums. This wasn't a storm in some far corner of the world. This was right here. The people he was talking about could be friends or neighbours.

"One boy was found drowned in a flash-flooded gully near the Oliver Pool," the reporter said.

Polly stood beside the television, her arms gripping her elbows tightly. "Could that be Chris?" she whispered.

"Two seniors were injured in a traffic accident at Kingsway Garden Mall. The tents in the mall parking lot where Art in the Garden was just wrapping up have blown down. Chairs, tables, and empty cartons have blown across the expanse of empty asphalt. Vandals have already struck, taking advantage of the confusion, smashing car windows and headlights on several parked vehicles." In one of the video shots, a small group of people in black raced across the parking lot away from what looked like the security guard in a gigantic parka.

"We better get over to the mall." Kyle shut the TV off with the remote control. Erin came through the door, wearing dry sneakers and a pair of long pants. "Mom and Constable Joe have gone to help set up an emergency shelter at the Oliver School gym. This is the worst area hit in the city."

"There's a kid dead. A young boy." Polly pulled on her slicker, grabbed a water bottle. Kyle ran and put a note on his parents' door telling them where he was.

The three of them slipped out the back and tiptoed past the downed willow. Polly felt tears close to her eyes. How totally vulnerable she felt, like a baby. Where was

Chris? What if the three of them in the tree fort hadn't wakened up? Who was the drowned boy? She fingered the sketchbook in her pocket, rolled the pencil in her right pocket beside the keys to her apartment. Too many unanswered questions rolled around in her head. She preferred innocence to this panic and sense of being responsible to her friends and community. What could one kid do?

"I'm scared," Kyle's voice squeaked.

Polly nodded.

"Move slowly," Erin said calmly.

"Right," Kyle answered. Wind from the north blew their way. Polly pulled her slicker hood up. The rain was slanted downwards, sharp and fine, like thousands of needles pricking her face.

The lights at the corner of the Kingsway and 109th Street weren't working. A traffic cop steered the few cars around a giant elm that had taken the light out and crashed across half of the intersection.

"Unbelievable," Erin murmured.

"Chaos," Kyle said.

"Look at that!" Polly pointed across the barren parking lot to where the two tents had stood. Two flood-lights and lights from passing cars revealed a desolate scene. All that remained were piles of nylon and canvas, a few aluminum pieces of framework, two dilapidated semi-trailers, and a dry ice van with heaps of dry ice steaming on the ground. Two smashed cars sat in the middle of a nearly deserted parking lot. A cluster of vehicles crowded by the main entrance to the mall. Two yellow school buses and an emergency response truck were pulled up right in front.

"I can't believe it," Polly headed toward one of the smashed cars, an ancient black Volkswagen. She crouched down and studied the broken headlights. Under the front of the car lay a hammer and some garbage.

"Let me see that," Kyle asked. He hefted the hammer. "Heavy." He turned it over and over. It had a red mark on the handle, nearly worn off. "B.S. 12/98, St. A."

"Someone isn't very polite," Erin said.

"I don't think those letters spell something bad," Kyle chuckled. "I think they are the initials of the owner, when he got the hammer and where he lives."

"Of course." Polly thought about the way her folks used initials and numbers to mark phone calls and important data. "Good work, Kyle."

She showed him the scraps of garbage that had been littering the ground. "Are you thinking what I'm thinking?"

Kyle nodded. He stared at the empty fries container from Soda Jerks in St. Albert. "Springstune from St. Albert, right."

Erin looked from Polly to Kyle and back again. "I'll just tag along."

A sudden gust of wind blew rain their way. They sprinted for the entrance.

There, sitting in the food fair, were all the people from the mall stores, the artists, and the volunteers. They looked exhausted. The mall music wasn't working, so it was very quiet, as if everyone had run out of words and music. The leftover odours of cinnamon buns, giant cookies, Chinese food, and coffee competed for attention from Polly's heightened sense of smell. "I'm hungry and I don't know why."

"Over here, Polly," Isabel called from a table near the New York Fries booth. "How are things outside?" Polly, Kyle, and Erin made their way over to the table. Mr. Russell, the volunteer co-ordinator, young Mike Payne, and Isabel were sitting together.

"Have you seen Peter Bianco or Chris?" Polly pulled up a white plastic chair.

"Peter, Maeve, and some of the others are still at the gallery," Mike said. "I came to check on Isabel. She's fine. She's a real trooper. Just like my uncle."

"He'll be home next week," Isabel said, "I got this young man a key to his uncle's place. He's going to move in and keep an eye on old Mike. I rescued your brother's sleeping bag."

"He's coming back next week," Polly said.

"Sorry about that." Mike hung his head. "Some nights it was pretty cold on that couch on the back porch."

"He's really one of the good guys," Isabel said proudly.

Polly chuckled. "You draw great magpies, Mike."

"Isabel's going to see if she can help me get into Grant McEwan College in the art and design program." The grin on young Mike's face was wider than Chris's, Polly thought.

"I've got to find Chris," she said. She didn't want to tell anyone that her head had flipped to the dead kid in the gully by Oliver pool. What if Chris had taken his sleeping bag and gone to the pool? Of course, it would be closed. Then what would he have done?

Polly started running down the silent corridor, past the art and pottery displays, the dried-flower arrangements, the handmade jewellery, slowing as she stared down the corridor to Sears. The doors to the big department store were locked. A table with sale flyers sat in front of the chained gates. She had been heading to her dad's Excel Sports store without thinking. He wasn't there. Polly turned, ran past the drugstore and the camera shop. On her left, across from the Wizard's Lair, lights blazed from the Starving Artist Gallery/Café. A cluster of people flowed in and out, steaming cups of coffee in their hands. A few smokers huddled outside the back entrance to the mall, puffing. The rain threatened to put out their cigarettes.

Peter Bianco stood in the centre of a group of admiring artists. They were all dressed in black with dangling or stud earrings in ears, noses, lips, and who knows where else on their bodies. She looked for someone who was missing an earring. It was like hunting for a needle in a haystack. She couldn't see anyone without a hole somewhere, but they were all filled. No missing earrings.

Man, maybe being innocent was just fine. Polly liked her body intact. She didn't want it pierced, poked, tattooed or tortured. The Untouched and Untattooed McDoodle laughed.

"Where's Chris?" she interrupted the conversation.

"He was here earlier," Peter said. "I thought he went home. He made some pretty snippy comments."

"He told his father that he was sick of being ignored. I know exactly how he feels." Maeve glared at Peter. "He wanted his mother. He said the people he thought were his friends weren't and it was Peter's fault." Maeve shook her head. "He didn't even look at his dad's pictures."

"He's just a kid," Polly said. "Give him a break."

"I asked him why it was my fault," Peter said.

"He said it was because Peter hadn't taught him any rules," Maeve said.

"I don't get it with the rules bit. I don't like rules," Peter said. "The whole of society is run by too many rules. Artists don't like rules."

"Right on," Josh said. Bruce nodded. He shoved six enormous french fries coated with ketchup in his mouth. "Society stinks."

"Some rules are necessary," Erin said quietly. She and Kyle had caught up with Polly and stood together, catching their breath. "We don't want people hurting others."

Polly was glad to see them, glad to have them on-board. They made a good team. She didn't want to do this alone.

"Sometimes you have to hurt people to make them understand." said Maeve. "My friends in the Dragon-flies believe that." Polly didn't like the glare Maeve was aiming at Peter Bianco. "Trashing stuff may be art too," she hissed.

Polly shook her head, wanting to tell these people they were insensitive louts. She didn't quite have the nerve. "Oh, forget all this stupid talking," Polly muttered. "This is serious. No one knows where Chris is. He's lost."

Peter Bianco put down his coffee, gulped twice. "In the storm?"

"We don't know," said Polly. "We've got to find him."

12. Lost in the Storm

"LET'S NOT PANIC," KYLE SAID. "WE KNOW HE'S NOT in his apartment or the tree fort."

"Where else does he go?" asked Erin.

"The pool, the playground, and the mall." Polly was staring at one of Peter Bianco's paintings. It showed a family group, sitting in what looked like a terminal. "He wouldn't have tried to run away, would he? Maybe go to a bus station or airport?"

"He only has two dollars," Peter said.

"Kids don't know how much tickets cost," Erin said. "It's a definite possibility."

"I'm just afraid he would go with anyone who acted friendly," Kyle said. "Polly says he's pretty trusting."

The more Polly thought about it, the less she worried about Chris being drowned. He didn't like being alone. He liked being near other people. There wouldn't have been other people around the pool in this weather. He wouldn't want to walk that far by himself. She was really sorry about that other kid, but it wouldn't be Chris. She still wanted to find him, though – to make sure he was safe.

"Should we call the police?" Peter asked. He looked really flustered, his hands moving in circles, fists clenching and unclenching as if he was trying to wrestle with an invisible enemy.

"I don't know," Polly said. "They are busy with accidents, fallen trees, and flooding. We should start looking ourselves."

"But if they heard about any lost kids they'd know enough to get a hold of us. Check if it's Chris." Erin stared around at the assembled crowd. "Peter should call the police. One team should inform security at the bus, train, and plane terminals to be on the lookout for an eight-year-old kid...."

"Alone or with a stranger," Polly shivered. The dumb kid would go with anyone. If only the three of them hadn't let him go off for snacks when he was angry.

"Why don't we all help find Chris?" Erin asked.

"Leave your stuff here, guys," Peter said. "Mandy will watch it." The twins put down their backpacks.

"Check back in an hour...unless there's news," Maeve added. "We'll get our stuff and hang out together."

"Hopefully we can put Chris to bed and party at my place," Peter added.

Polly dug out her sketchbook and flipped the pages. Mike and Peter headed toward the pay phones. Maeve and a couple of other artists took her old beater of a car and pictures of Chris and headed to the bus and train stations. There was the International Airport but they didn't think he could make it out there on his own. Three bike riders promised to check the neighbourhood parks and the Oliver pool. With the storm blowing over they could skirt any dangerous areas. Polly handed each team one of her preliminary sketches of Chris Bianco.

Kyle took one of her best sketches, the one of Chris standing near the mural waving his small flag. He wrote 'Missing Child" across the bottom in black marker from Polly's pencil case. He stared around the now nearly empty gallery. A row of backpacks, satchels, and art folios leaned behind the counter. Obviously the belongings of all the search teams.

"Have you any tape?" he asked the skinny girl behind the counter. Mandy was sitting on a high wrought iron and glass stool. She frowned at him as if all younger kids were a nuisance, as if being stuck here all night was a nuisance. She must have thought she was an artist too, because she was wearing a shiny silk black skirt that came to her ankles and black shiny platform heels that looked a foot high.

She shrugged her shoulders and went back to reading a teen magazine, plugged into headphones. The music sounded tinny and distant.

The mall was very quiet. Like a sleeping giant. No one seemed to be around. Of course it must be after midnight. Polly was surprised how wide awake she was. "My head is buzzing."

"It's the flow of adrenaline in your system. We've had several traumatic shocks," Kyle said. "Our primordial ancestors needed this fight-or-flight mechanism to be working well if they were going to survive."

"Thanks for those words of wisdom," Polly said. Maybe that was the way Kyle dealt with bad things. She drew. He got intellectual. "Practically speaking, Kyle, what do we need to do?"

"We need tape to put up posters. There's a photocopy

machine in the all-night drug store.

"We could buy tape." Erin held up her wallet.

"Or check for a roll." Polly pointed to the row of backpacks.

"Isn't that stealing?" Erin asked. "We hunt for crooks, we don't become like them."

"You're right," Polly sighed. She remembered how she had felt when Chris had tried to take over the fort and spilled her markers.

"We'll buy some tape," Kyle said. "However we might spot a clue or two on the outside – like initials. Everyone's stuff is here."

Erin said, "I'm not digging into other people's stuff. I wouldn't want anyone digging into my backpack. I'm willing to check the names. You're right, Kyle, everyone's stuff is here."

"Except for Harold's," Polly said. "We're pretty sure he didn't take the art supplies or smash the cars. He's a security guard."

"And old enough to know better," Erin said. She bent over one of the satchels, staring at the name embossed on the top. Kyle peered into a bright orange bag in the centre. A small card was fastened in a plastic holder – "Michael S. Payne, Jr." it said. A laughing magpie filled the rest of the card. "If we had seen this sooner, we would have known who the Graffiti Ghost was." Kyle headed off toward the drugstore to buy tape and copy signs.

"We'll catch up in a minute," Polly hollered after him. Her voice echoed down the deserted marble and glass corridor.

"What's this?" Erin pointed to a black satchel, gaping open. "It's sure looks heavy." She gazed up and down the hallway and over at the girl with her Walkman plugged in, propped on the stool behind the counter, oblivious to everything.

Polly joined her. They studied the satchel. It was worn leather with scrapes and scratches, and one corner looked like it might break. Brass initials were embossed on the top flap – B.S. An array of tools for metalwork, plus a small crowbar and some beat-up cans of spray paint stuck out of the top. A large plastic Baggie with ketchup, vinegar, mustard packets, spoons, and salt and peppers from fast food places was jammed into a side pocket.

Beside the black satchel was a black plastic case. J.S. was scrawled in white paint on the rough surface. It was wrapped in a leather belt with a lock.

"The Springstune boys, I gather," Polly said. "Looks as if they are heavily into deconstruction rather than art."

"They sound totally cynical." The two girls hurried down the corridor to catch up with Kyle. "Keeping bad company. Not like us – we stay with folks with a positive attitude." Erin whistled a happy tune as she ran.

Polly smiled, thinking of the change in Erin from last spring. She hadn't been very friendly or positive back then, but that was another story, wasn't it? The point was, Erin was in a good space now.

Kyle had made twenty copies of the poster, putting both Peter's cellphone number and the McDougall's cell number on the bottom of the page. "I wonder if Peter's home phone is back on yet?"

"I doubt if he's had a chance to pay the bill," Polly said.

Their footsteps echoed as they made their way along

each corridor of the mall. Harold's night replacement waved from near Sears. A cleaning person was trying to scrub a spray-painted swastika off the wall near the washrooms. The paint was thick and globby.

"It's really late – nearly the middle of the night," Kyle whispered as if the mirrors or store windows might be spying. He put a poster on a Thrifty's store window. "I've never been up all night, have you?"

Polly's cellphone rang. "Any luck at your end?" Peter asked.

"We've posted signs," Polly said. "The mall is quiet."

"The police have issued an all-points bulletin. They are worried that some kooky person might have picked him up." Peter paused. "They were pretty mad at me for not keeping better tabs on him, Polly."

"Well, you tried." Polly didn't want to say that she agreed with the police.

"I guess I forgot how little he really is."

Polly didn't know what to say to the distraught father.

"We're going to drive up and down the blocks around the mall and between the apartment and the playground."

"We're checking out every corner of the mall," Polly said.

"Shouldn't you kids be in bed?" Peter asked.

Polly shook her head furiously "no," then realized that Peter couldn't see her. "We're in this with you, Peter. After all, he ran away because of the rules I put in my sketchbook."

"Maybe I need to see those rules, Polly, when you get a chance." Peter paused. "I left that to Chao. Until she gets back, I guess I've got to be both the rule maker and the game player."

Polly could hear his rattly old van moving slowly down some street as he talked.

"A lot of chaos and confusion out here. There's a crowd on the next corner, close to the pocket park. We'll go and check it out. I'll check with you in a little while." Peter hung up.

Polly put the cellphone back in her pocket. She pulled out her sketchbook and opened it to the great picture she had done of the tree fort only a couple of weeks ago. Little did she know back then how few days the fort had left before.... Her mind went blank, as if it was filled with snow, as if there were no pictures left to draw, only chaos and disorder. Would the world ever right itself?

She sat beside her two friends on a wide marble bench outside the all-night drugstore. They leaned on each other for support.

"I'm feeling pretty miserable," Polly confessed. "I'm stumped. Things couldn't be any worse if they tried. Some detectives we are."

Kyle sighed loudly but didn't say anything.

"I'm so tired I can't think straight," Erin said.

"What are we going to do now?" Polly asked. The Depressed and Despairing McDoodle stared at the shiny tile floor as if it would give her an answer. If she couldn't think her way out of this, she might just as well give up being a detective, let alone a friend to younger kids. Oh, Chris, where are you?

13. Turning a Corner

A CASH REGISTER DRAWER CLANGED IN THE DRUGSTORE, startling Polly from her near sleep. She forced her eyes open wide and stared at Gladys as she swished out of the store in her pink tracksuit. She had a small bag of toiletries clutched in her hand.

"Harold has to stay in hospital for a few days," she said when she saw the three kids. "He had been overdoing it, you know."

"Can we go and see him?" Polly asked politely.

"It's the middle of the night, you know."

"Tomorrow?"

"Oh, right, tomorrow." Gladys heaved a huge sigh. "This storm, this arts festival, it's been too much for him, you know."

"We know," Polly said.

"I'm taking him to meet my family in Seattle as soon as he's well enough to travel, you know."

"I didn't know you were from Seattle, you know." Polly shook her head. She'd have to wake up and stop repeating all the "you knows" Gladys said. She nearly giggled, but when she thought about Harold in hospital, Chris missing, and the storm she pushed the laughter away. It was probably a sign of nerves anyway. "Is Harold all right?"

"They were afraid it was his heart, you know. Turned out he hadn't been eating proper for a diabetic," Gladys said. "That man needs someone to look after him."

And you want the job, Polly thought. She remembered Gladys sitting knitting while they all waited for the ceremony to start that would honour Isabel and her mural. Harold had looked pretty seedy. Polly had thought it had something to do with his guilt – not about smashing the mural – no not that, McDoodle and Clay were pretty sure that wasn't his style – more that he had seen someone else doing it and had been glad, maybe hadn't moved as fast as he could, maybe couldn't move as fast as he wanted. He'd certainly investigated it, gotten paint flecks on his new security guard suit, hadn't he – not dandruff, never dandruff. Polly sighed loudly. People were fascinating, a real mixture of good and bad. Even old people had to make tough decisions. Maybe she really had been awfully innocent for a city kid. This summer was teaching her too many lessons – tough ones.

After Gladys had disappeared toward the nearest exit, Polly took her sketchbook out of the bottom of her backpack. She flipped back to sketches of the opening. She had a sketch of Isabel's face, Mike's face, Harold's sad worried frown, and one of Chris chasing a jawbreaker under the stage. The red curtains were flung about and his slight, wiggly body scurried from under the stage, reminding Polly of a zealous dog who had rescued a tasty bone.

Reminding Polly of how much Chris liked hidden cozy places.

"Come on you guys," she cried. "We've got work to do."

Polly lifted the skirts of the nearest stall and stared under a table that had pottery displayed. Boxes and a coat lay on the floor, hidden by the red skirt. "I wonder...."

"You wonder what?" asked Erin as she posted a sign on a dress shop window.

Without saying a word, Polly raced down the corridor, turned at the corner, and headed toward the mural. Sure enough, the bleachers and stage were still set up. Workmen had not had a chance to pull them down yet.

She stopped and waited for Kyle and Erin to catch up with her. For some reason, she was afraid to look under the stage. She was afraid of what she might or might not find. Afraid for Chris and Peter. She needed company with her to do this. She needed her team. Her heart was pounding like the hailstones in the parking lot behind the apartment. No, no it was the footfalls of her two buddies as they came around the corner. Polly bent down and walked slowly around the skirted stage.

A small wedge of midnight-blue padded material with stars and planets on it stuck out from underneath the red curtain, right close to the far corner nearest the magpie on the mural. A strong smell of pizza and popcorn came from that corner as well.

"Chris, are you under there?" she cried, falling on her knees and lifting the curtain simultaneously. A Mr. Pizza box, a nearly empty carton of popcorn with a few pieces trailing, led towards a curled-up figure rolled in a sleeping bag, his head on a Mickey Mouse pillowcase.

"Whaaat?" a sleepy voice responded.

Kyle and Erin stood behind Polly, their breath sounding raspy like low thunder. "You found him."

"Polly, is that you? Did you come looking for me? Are we friends again, are we?" A very welcome, but very sleepy sounding voice quizzed her.

"Yes, we are." Polly pulled the kid out from under the stage and gave him a giant hug until he squirmed to get away. "Take it easy, okay? What's all the fuss?" His innocent eyes stared up at Polly, over at Erin and Kyle. "I was going to come wake you up in the morning. I ran away."

"We noticed," Erin said.

"You gave everyone a real scare," Kyle said.

"Why? I knew where I was," Chris said. "Are you mad at me?"

Polly shook her head and sighed. "Your dad and all his friends are out looking for you. We've been posting signs."

"Are they? Are they really?"

"There was a really bad storm. When you weren't in the tree fort or your apartment...."

"I got mad at Daddy and you guys," Chris said. "I wanted to go find my mom, but I only had two dollars. So I bought a small pizza instead. Some old guy gave me popcorn but was mad when I wouldn't go with him for a ride in his car."

Erin gasped, "You could have been kidnapped."

"One of Polly's rules said, *choose your friends wisely,*" Chris replied. "I didn't know him. I kept the popcorn though. Was that bad?"

Polly was out of breath, as if she had just run a

marathon. "Not bad. So you ran away to the mall?"

Chris nodded his head ten times like the doll with the spring in its neck. It made Polly feel queasy inside, thinking of all the bad things that could have happened and hadn't.

Kyle frowned. "You ran away to the mall?"

"I feel safe here. There's lots of people and I know where everything is."

"I like the lake," Erin reflected. "The outdoors."

"I run away to books," Kyle said. "Polly draws."

None of them seemed to know how to talk. It was as if finding Chris had made them all dippy. Polly figured they were in shock. She really felt like screaming with relief – dancing a jig or climbing a mountain – and she didn't even like sports.

"We have to let the police and everyone else know we've found Chris." Polly tried Peter's cellphone. The line was busy. She picked up the Star Trek sleeping bag and headed toward the exit. "Let's go home."

STANDING IN THE GLARE of two sets of car headlights and the apartment floodlight, the three young detectives discovered a small crowd surveying the damage to the tree, car, and fort, shaking their heads in disbelief. Chris ran and jumped into his father's arms. "I'm found. I'm found. Polly found me. I didn't know I was lost, but she found me."

Tears sparkled in Peter's eyes as he thanked Polly. "It's time this chap got to bed – and the rest of us as well."

"Thank goodness," Maeve said. "We were just heading over to the gallery to check in when we saw Peter and Mike in the van turning in here."

Erin checked her watch. "Someone should alert the others."

Kyle nodded.

Mike Payne and the two artists who had been with Maeve stood talking about the damaged car and the repairs needed. Polly shook her head – they seemed more concerned with the smashed vehicle than with young Chris, who was holding fast to his dad's hand. A small group of neighbours had gathered in the yard and were busy picking through the trashed fort and staring at the car. Long sighs and low conversations followed.

"We'll go over and pick up our backpacks and stuff," Maeve said, heaving a big sigh of relief. She collected her two sidekicks. "Unless you need me here, Peter?" She looked hopeful.

"No. But could you bring my backpack? I can't leave Chris." Peter added, "Let poor Mandy go home." Mike Payne asked Maeve to bring his backpack too.

Maeve nodded. "Tomorrow should be fabulous at the mall after the storm. Everyone will be there." She pushed her hair back from her face. "Oh, dang, I've lost an earring." She looked down to the ground.

Polly bent to help her. "What did it look like?"

"I make them myself," Maeve said. "I need better butterfly clips. I lost one of my best designs yesterday as well. I should check the floor of the gallery."

"Did it look like this?" Polly felt in her pocket and brought out the dragonfly earring.

"Where'd you find this?" Maeve asked. "It might be mine. But I made four or five – for a group of boys I knew who wanted matching earrings."

"Hang out with them, do you?" Polly asked. "The Dragonflies?"

"Sometimes," Maeve said cautiously. "I've got lots of friends at the mall, not just Peter. He's old and married."

"And unavailable, right?" Polly looked over at the father and son busy talking, their tousled heads side by side, Peter crouched down listening intently to what Chris was saying. It might have taken a crisis, but it looked as if the Biancos were getting their act together.

"I'll take the earring, thanks." Maeve reached out her hand and grabbed the delicate silver dragonfly. She turned and strode to her car. She and the two artists piled in and she drove away, splattering gravel and rain-water as they disappeared down the dark lane.

"Where does Maeve go when she's not here?" Erin wondered.

"I've seen her with the Dragonflies," said Peter. "They're pretty rough guys, though." Polly, Kyle, and Erin nodded.

"One looks like he needs a shave, one has masses of pimples. They look greasy and grey," Polly said. "Not your typical teens, thank goodness."

"Smell of cigarettte smoke and liquor, I bet." Erin shuddered. Peter shook his head sadly. "I hate it that some young people drink too early and too much."

"Me too," Polly added. She gulped thinking about how her friend had been robbed of a father.

The parking lot was slowly emptying of bystanders. Peter Bianco moved his van out of the middle of the lot to a spot with no debris in it from the tree fort and pocketed his keys. Mike Payne hesitated. "I guess I'll come up for a bit, Peter, before I go and crash at my uncle's house. Maeve will be bringing our backpacks. Some of the other artists may show up here."

"I don't feel much like a party, after all," Peter said. "Why don't you come in, Mike? You can help me thank the searchers and send them away."

"Maeve too?"

"Especially Maeve," Peter said. "I've got some real serious thinking to do."

"Can we call Mommy, can we?" Chris asked his father as the two of them headed for the back door of the apartment. His father nodded.

The sky was already lightening. Dawn would soon come in northern Alberta. A few early birds were already discussing noisily the problems of broken branches and fallen trees.

"Do you want to come up for snacks?" Kyle asked. "Mom and Dad will be sleeping by now."

"We need to get to bed," Erin said.

"Enough excitement for one night." Polly followed Erin up to her apartment. The two girls didn't even take off their Art in the Garden T-shirts before they fell asleep.

14. Calm After the Storm

LATE THE NEXT MORNING, ERIN, POLLY, AND KYLE sat down to a brunch of pancakes, sausages, orange juice, and bananas in yogurt. Rachel Darby sipped coffee as she supervised the electric grill. Outside the window, city trucks and repair crews patrolled the streets. Gas and electricity crews were out in full force. Some areas of the city were still without power. The insurance company rep was coming by to see about the cars damaged in the storm.

"What are we going to do about the tree fort?" Polly stacked three pieces of pancake on her fork, moved the banana and yogurt away from the pool of syrup. She didn't like mixing her food.

The doorbell rang. Peter and Chris Bianco stood outside. "Here's where you are," Chris said. "Kyle's mom said you might be here. Are you eating? We came to say goodbye."

"And thanks," Peter said. "We're going to Vancouver."

"In that old van?" Kyle asked.

Peter nodded. "I can fix almost anything."

"What about the kids in the mall?" Polly asked. What about us?

"We called Mommy. She'd been trying to get us for two days. The phone has been off. She's flying to Vancouver tomorrow. Said she read my e-mail. Said she wanted to see us really bad. We can pick her up there. Have a big reunion." Chris was blathering again. It made Polly chuckle. He had recovered from last night's ordeal. Of course, he'd slept through most of it, and as he had said, he had known where he was all the time.

"Maybe we'll move there," Peter said. "We could start over."

"Is Vancouver closer to Hong Kong?" Chris bounced up and down on his untied sneakers. His cow T-shirt was clean but wrinkled. The cow looked like it was dancing a jig.

"What about the apartment?" Polly asked.

"Oh, I've packed anything we really want. We've got it in the van already." Peter sounded nearly as young as his kid. "It will be great to see Chao again. We can be a family."

"We'll have to go over to the mall and take down the signs," Erin said. "This kid has definitely been found."

"I sure have, haven't I?"

Rachel offered Peter and Chris brunch. They tucked into a big stack of pancakes. The two of them played a game of name the shape in the pancake.

"It looks like a dinosaur to me," said Chris.

"What kind?" His father grinned. The two heads leaned together over the plate swimming in syrup.

"A stegosaurus."

"Right on," Peter said. "Now it's your turn."

Chris giggled as he carved up a pancake. "You'll never guess."

Polly watched as the father and son played with each other, forgetting everyone around them. Maybe having a father who was like a big kid wasn't so bad. Especially when he played with you. Polly shook her head. She'd been finishing one of the sketches of Chris in her sketchbook, the one with him in the tree fort. She noticed that the list she had made of all the rules for kids was missing from her sketchbook. Polly wondered when the little tyke had taken it. Maybe he was going to be all right in the long run.

By the end of the day, with the work crew in the backyard and Peter and Chris on the road, everything would be different. She might never see them again. A lump formed in her throat, as she thought of all the time over the last few weeks she had spent either being with Chris or worrying about him.

"Here, I want you to have this," Polly blushed as she handed the Biancos the finished sketch of Chris in the tree fort. "I'm not as good an artist as your father or Isabel."

"You've got a real quick hand with a pencil," Peter Bianco said.

"What about the rules?" Chris asked. "I tore that page out last night. It might come in handy. Are the rules the same in Vancouver? Are they?"

Peter stared around the room as if he expected to see them on the wall. Rachel and Erin's apartment was tidy and sparsely furnished, but had some interesting pieces of pottery, sculpture, and weaving from their relatives.

"Polly wrote a bunch of rules for me. She was hoping

to teach me a thing or two."

"Maybe I shouldn't have." Polly's head drooped.

"You never did tell him Rule Number Ten, Polly," Erin said.

"Oh, oh," Chris moaned, "I'm not sure I want to hear."

"It's the best of all," Polly lifted her head and looked straight into the younger kid's sparkling eyes. "It said something like – remember you are a very important person, a VIP, and you have friends." Impulsively Polly hugged both Biancos.

"That's a pretty good rule," Peter Bianco chuckled. "We could all use that one." He paused a moment. "Thanks for taking care of Chris. I'm not much good at running a house by myself. Chris has promised not to run away again."

They both thanked Rachel Darby for the delicious brunch. Polly discovered she, the Overemotional and Overzealous McDoodle, was close to crying. Kyle took the plate from in front of her to the sink. Erin started humming one of Isabel Ashton's old songs, "I'll be Seeing You," as she loaded the dishwasher. Then Polly, Kyle, and Erin helped the Biancos load their van, and waved as they drove off.

"Say goodbye to all the young artists," Peter said. "I'll be back to pick up my paintings. Did I tell you I sold two? We've got cash in our jeans." He grinned, gunned his noisy motor, and drove off.

"You know," Polly said as they went back inside to do the dishes, "I'm part sorry and part glad about Chris. I'd gotten used to him. But kids need parents." She thought back to when her mom had yelled at her about her untidy room and stewed about where she would stay while she and Dad were away. She pictured her dad loading the pizza with mushrooms and peppers while the rest of the family supervised. Life evened out somehow.

After she had finished scrubbing the grill, she went to the patio, leaned out, and looked down the lane on the off chance that her parents might be coming. Her thumbs itched – maybe she was psychic or some part of her brain had heard their car motor. They drove up. She ran down to meet them.

Kyle slipped on his sandals. He'd been reading the Saturday comics. "We need to go over to the mall and take down those signs."

Downstairs, the McDougalls stood staring at the mess in the parking lot.

"It's hard to believe a storm could do that much damage. We didn't have anything but a centimetre of rain in Red Deer." Jan McDougall shook her head sadly. "I thought about you all night, Polly."

"I'm sure glad you guys moved inside," Polly's dad gave her a big hug. "We were worried."

Polly nodded, received a brisk hug from her mother and chuckled to herself about how every family had its specialities. "I'm glad you're home," is all she said out loud. I'm your kid and whatever happens we can handle it.

"We need to go over to the mall and take down the signs," Kyle said again. "Are you coming?"

"Yes," Polly said. "I want to check a few things, talk to a few people."

"Wait for me," Erin called from her balcony. "I'll be right down."

The three of them looked both ways as they crossed the Kingsway. The traffic lights weren't working yet, so there was a cop waving people through the intersection. Tree branches littered the boulevard by the new RCMP building, and an abandoned car with a shattered windshield and right front fender waited on the curbside for a tow truck.

"I MISSED YOU GUYS," Polly said. "Now life can get back to normal."

"We were only away a couple of weeks," Kyle said.

"It felt longer." Erin nodded her head. She had borrowed her mother's Tilley hat to keep the sun off. It shaded her dark eyes.

"Things got pretty hectic around the apartment building and the mall after Peter and Chris moved in. They were a bit of a tornado in their own right. I've gotten used to talking everything through with you guys."

"The trouble was, you had too many mysteries to work on all at once," Erin said. "Now we only have one."

"I'm glad Mike Payne found Mike Payne. The Graffiti Ghost turned out to be a harmless neighbour with an itchy artistic hand." Kyle headed across the mall parking lot to the rebuilt bus shelter. A giant pine tree leaned across it precariously, and a magpie nest from the pine's branches sat on top of the bus shelter. Three magpies strutted, squawked, and bullied the onlookers. Two guys in a city truck sat staring at the leaning pine, scratching their heads. "Looks like we're not the only ones who got an eviction notice," Kyle said.

A crew was cleaning up the mess caused when the stage and giant tent had collapsed. Two dumpsters sat beside the entrance to the mall. Torn canvas, bent aluminum strips, frayed ropes, and soggy cardboard filled the dumpsters to the brim.

Polly watched as some of the teenaged volunteers from Art in the Garden hauled more debris and put it in the back of a pickup truck. Mike Payne the younger, Maeve, and a few others that Polly recognized were working away.

"Where are Bruce and Josh?" asked Polly as she approached Maeve. "I think we have a hammer of Bruce's."

"Quite the storm, eh? Did you see the size of the hailstones?" Mike jumped down from the back of the truck where he had been organizing things. "I was glad I slept inside last night. The porch is soaking."

"I never heard where Chris was last night," Maeve said.

Polly and Kyle were staring at the debris as if it might answer some questions they had.

"He slept in the mall," Erin said.

"Where are Peter and Chris?" asked Mike. "I wanted to take them in to meet my uncle. He hasn't had many visitors. I would have gone, but I didn't know he was there. Thanks to Isabel, Kyle, and Polly, who figured out who I was and who my uncle was."

Polly giggled. No wonder Mike drew magpies. He chattered like one now that he was settled. "Peter and Chris have left for B.C. Chris's mother is coming in from Hong Kong. Evidently she got the e-mail I sent her from Chris and decided she had been away long enough."

"Peter's left for B.C.!" Maeve screamed. "Without even saying goodbye to me! What a jerk! What a thoughtless pain in the...." She turned and ran across the parking lot to her old car and drove away.

Just then, Isabel came over to the little group.

"Well, well, Polly McDoodle. Thanks to you, a lot of stuff is getting sorted out, I'd say." Isabel joined the group by the dismantled tent. "I was just heading over to McDonald's for lunch. Anyone want to come?"

"We just finished brunch," Kyle said, "but some fries would taste good."

The whole bunch walked across the parking lot, veering to miss the downed pine tree and displaced magpies. A panel truck was in line for takeout. Bruce and Josh were sitting in the truck beside a thickset grey-haired man with no neck and black sunglasses. "Springer's Metalworks, St. Albert," the sign on the door said.

"Looks like we're losing a couple of suspects." Polly darted through the parked cars to the side of the truck. "Don't forget your hammer." The two boys acted as if they didn't know her. Then she flipped open her sketch-book to the pencil drawing of the smashed car. Out of her pocket she pulled a plastic Baggie, five empty ketchup packets, and two vinegar ones. "Mr. Springer, I think you need to ask your kids what they've been doing here at the mall."

The older guy took his order from the window – burgers, drinks, and large fries complete with stacks of ketchup and vinegar packets. He handed the tray of food to Bruce. Then he pulled the van out of traffic and parked at the edge of the lot, closest to the mall.

"What's all this about?" he asked, getting out of his truck and coming around. "I've been out of town on business. The boys said they were working on a metal sculpture in the park. We were just going to see it. Why don't you hop in?"

The whole crew piled in the van and Mr. Springer drove to the pocket park at the end of the lane by Polly's apartment. There in the centre of a gravel pad stood the pile of bent aluminum, cans, pipes, motor parts, and shopping cart, molded and bolted together. "Urban Deconstruction" was written on a metal plaque – by Bruce and Josh Springer. A litter bag nearby had scads of empty ketchup and vinegar packets.

The two boys hung their heads. "We got carried away. When the parks supervisor said we could do a sculpture, we went to junkyards, scarfed things from neighbours," Bruce said. "We even followed some vandals around to pick up broken bits."

Josh nodded. "We never took anything that wasn't already banged up."

"We'd been having a bad summer. Mom is away. Then Dad had to go away on business. We decided to hang out in the mall in Edmonton where no one knew us. That's where we met Peter Bianco." Bruce took a breath.

"We met some guys who were really into bad trips. They smoked and drank and agreed with us that life was a bummer."

"Peter told us we were too depressing, to lighten up," Josh said.

"So we went off with those other guys," Bruce added. "The Dragonflies."

"The trouble was, they started banging things, smashing windows and laughing about it. We saw them smash Isabel's mural, Harold came along so they all ran away. But he saw us. We never figured out why he didn't tell. Then they started on junky cars. In some ways, we envied them. Fitted with the way we'd been thinking. Life is a bummer. Nobody cares."

"But we couldn't do it. Something stopped us," Bruce added.

"Maybe decency and common sense," their father said. "And having your parents home."

"You know the boys who did it, these Dragonflies?" Polly asked. "They dress in black...."

"And have matching earrings," Josh added. "Made by...." He stopped mid-sentence and blushed.

"Maeve," Kyle said.

"I didn't say that," Josh said. "I won't rat on a friend."

"I think we need to make a trip to the police station," the boys' father said. "You've got some things to talk about, some names to share."

"But Dad, all the cars were old."

"I don't care. You have to take responsibility for what you did and who you saw."

By this time, Polly was starving. "If I don't go and eat soon, I'll fade away to nothing, the Incredibly Shrinking McDoodle."

"Me too," added Kyle.

"First, my sons want to say something." Mr. Springer pushed the boys in Polly's direction.

"We didn't...I mean, we shouldn't have...." Josh stammered, standing in front of Kyle and Polly. "Things got out of hand, okay?" Bruce nodded in agreement.

Polly was still pretty upset, but she nodded. She shook hands with the father and his boys, turned and headed back to the fast food restaurant with Kyle by her side. She would leave the rest up to Mr. Springer. He and his sons finally got to eat their lunch, sitting in the park close to their sculpture. The two detectives left them there, sadder but wiser.

15. Life Goes On

IN MCDONALD'S, ISABEL HAD FOUND A GROUP OF tables away from the sunny windows. Kyle and Erin went for the food. Isabel, Mike, and Polly sat and talked things over.

"So Harold knew who had smashed the mural?" Isabel asked.

"But didn't tell," Mike said. "I may have drawn magpies, but I didn't hurt any of Isabel's art. I just wanted to let everyone know I was around. I was perfectly prepared to have the magpie disappear under another coat of paint."

"During the Second World War, we had a rash of graffiti. 'Kilroy was here!' was plastered, painted, and sprayed everywhere. No one ever got caught." Isabel took her tea bag out of her paper cup and laid it gently on the plastic cup cover as if it was a precious jewel. "Chaos and fear drive people to do many strange things."

Polly was flipping pages in her sketchbook. "I knew that something was funny when I spotted the flecks on Harold's shoulders. He had to have been poking around in the hole caused by the vandals. I didn't think he would do it. But he was glad it was done. He was jealous of Isabel."

"It's a good thing he's resigned as a security guard," Isabel said. "He's gone on disability. He and Gladys are going to go halfers on a RV. They're going to paint and quilt and travel – selling their wares as they go from one flea market to another." Isabel sighed. "He apologized when I went to visit him in the hospital."

"Chris thought he loved you," Polly said.

"Maybe so," Isabel said firmly. "But I didn't love him. Gladys may want to hang out with an old guy who is grumpy, but I don't."

Erin and Kyle arrived with the food. Everyone dove in and for a couple of minutes there wasn't a sound except for slurping and chewing.

Polly was rarely content to have a long period of silence in a conversation. She wanted to get on with solving the crimes. "I wonder where Maeve went?" She shoved her french fries away from her half-eaten hamburger.

"Maeve's probably over at the mall, hanging out. After all it is Saturday afternoon. Prime time." Kyle sucked on his double straw, making gurgling noises like a salivating monster.

"I'm just afraid she might be getting into trouble." Polly wiped her greasy fingers on a napkin. "She was pretty mad at Peter Bianco. When she gets mad, she does bad things." Polly flipped the pages of her sketchbook to a line drawing of Maeve at the swimming pool. She took a heavy black pencil and added a black ski hat pulled down over the forehead, baggy black jeans, and a black jacket. "I bet she's the smallest of the vandals who attacked the women with the jewellery and pottery counter. Let's go ask her."

"We'll finish up here," Isabel said. "Mike and I have some talking to do. I'm due at the mural by two p.m. I'm being interviewed by the *Edmonton Journal*. They're running a whole section on the Hudson's Bay Reserve in a couple of weeks. Alex Mair and Tony Cashman are supplying the historical material. I'm providing the art."

"I'll be over in a little while," Mike Payne said. "Maeve never did bring my backpack to Peter's."

"Let's go." Kyle tossed his trash in the container and joined Polly as she strode toward the mall. "We've still got work to do."

Traffic was really heavy. Repair crews were everywhere. Gawkers and visitors slowed to stare at each crumpled car, toppled tree, or damaged house. Police cruisers passed going both ways.

"There's Patrick Connelly." Polly waved frantically. The cruiser pulled over.

"Have you heard from Josh and Bruce yet?" she asked.

"Have you heard of a gang called the Dragonflies?" asked Erin.

"Have you found the vandals?" Kyle asked.

"Whoa," Officer Connelly said. "Do I gather that some concrete evidence, some irrefutable clues have been found?" He unfolded from the front passenger seat. The police radio was mumbling about emergencies in different areas of the city. The uniformed driver nodded hello. "So these are your favourite amateur detectives, Patrick?"

Polly shoved the sketchpad into the policeman's large hands. "We're going to check if that is one of the culprits."

"One of the ones who tipped over the jewellery display," added Erin.

"The small one." Kyle's voice creaked like a rusty door hinge. "That's a girl, not a boy."

"Her name is Maeve. She has a beat-up old car and hangs out with the Dragonflies," said Polly. "We thought she was a friend."

"She's not all bad," Kyle said. He held out a folded piece of paper to Patrick. "That's her license plate number. I noted it when she went out hunting for Chris last night."

"She just hung out with bad company," Erin said.

"Where are you kids going now?" Patrick asked. "You probably need to come into our local police station and report all this."

"We have to take the signs down." Kyle said.

"The ones about Chris being missing," Polly said. "Don't want to confuse people."

"We'll be by the mural before two o'clock," Polly said. "In case you want to talk to us some more."

The uniformed officer behind the wheel sounded the horn. Patrick hopped in and the cruiser sped away. Polly grinned. "The three of us peppered poor Patrick with information, didn't we?"

"That's what private investigators do," said Kyle. "Look at the horrendous job they have to do today. I bet catching a few vandals isn't uppermost in their minds."

"It is in mine," said Polly. She thought of the dismayed look on Isabel's face when she had seen the smashed mural. She thought of the tears of the jeweller. She thought of Peter's artwork in the gallery/café. "Let's go."

Every corridor of the mall was crowded with people. The noise level was really high. The excitement and fear caused by the storm seemed to have made everyone frantic. They weren't buying as much as strolling along, checking out the few artists' tables still erected down the centre of each hallway.

Polly and Erin made their way toward the jewellery kiosk close to Sears. Kyle took off looking for Maeve's car in one of the parking lots. They promised to meet by Isabel's mural before two o'clock.

"I think we should all go out to Small Shadow Lake tomorrow," said Kyle. "No matter what."

"Me too," said Erin. "I need some fresh air."

"Me three," chimed in Polly, the Friendly and Befriended McDoodle.

The potter recognized Polly, as the two girls approached the booth. She was busy packing up. She was tenderly wrapping clay birds in handmade nests of twigs.

Polly gasped. "It's my magpie." She pointed to a plump bird sitting on a real willow branch.

"How much is it?" asked Erin.

"For Polly?" the woman asked. "Let me think about it."

The customer who had been with the jeweller left. The brightly dressed artist came over, was introduced to Erin, and viewed Polly's sketchbook. "That's him. That's the little guy who knocked over my display. How did you know?"

"That's no guy," said Polly. "That's Maeve, the young jewellery maker. I suspect she was mad when you wouldn't let her sell some of her jewellery at your table. She got her friends in the Dragonflies to help her knock things over."

The potter stood listening, nodding her head. "You really are a detective, Polly."

Polly blushed. "I try."

The potter held out a wrapped box, just the size of a bird on a branch. "Erin and I want you to have this." She grinned.

Polly shook her head. "I can't take it. It's too much."

"That's for us to decide, Polly," said Erin. "I know how you like souvenirs of every case. This is a good one. It can go on the shelf in your room where the stuffed rabbit and the carved deer live."

Impulsively, Polly gave both Erin and the potter hugs. "Thanks."

As it was only shortly after one-fifteen, the girls ambled slowly down the corridor from Sears toward the food court. Polly's dad shouted from the Jiffy Coffee Shop. Polly gave him the magpie to keep safe in his store until closing time. He gave her a couple of dollars in case she had another hunger attack. He said business was really brisk and he was selling new sneakers as if everyone had decided to buy running equipment to get away from the effects of the storm.

"Take it easy, kid," he said as he headed down the corridor to the Excel store.

Erin and Polly nodded. They stood discussing the merits of buying an ice cream cone.

"Maeve's car is in the parking lot, just outside the far door, near the new gallery/café," hollered Kyle as he darted through the crowd. People turned and stared as he wove around family groups as if he was a quarterback with the football.

"Let's split up and try to spot her," Erin said.

"Wait! What do we do if we do find her?" asked Polly, remembering the trouble she'd gotten into the last time she tried catching crooks on her own.

"You guys hunt," said Kyle. "I'll find the police. They're mostly parked by the crashed bus shelter or on the other side by the downed tents. They can keep an eye on the car. That's where she'll go if she figures out we're after her."

"Oh, great!" Polly sighed.

"Take down the missing-kid signs near the gallery, will you?" Kyle asked Polly. "I think we put up two, but I'm not sure. Check with the girl at the counter."

"Do you want me to come with you?" asked Erin.

Polly shook her head, no. "Why don't you take down signs by the Food Fair and report to Isabel at the mural? Keep your eyes peeled all the way."

"Are you sure?" Erin asked. "You don't want company?"

Polly nodded again. She had walked into this whole mystery alone. Something inside told her she had to walk out of it by herself as well. She was the one who felt really mad and sad about the whole thing. Even if she couldn't do anything more, she had to walk these halls looking for the girl who had fooled her all that time. She ripped signs down and threw them in a garbage bin.

Polly turned into the corridor by the Starving Artists Gallery/Café. Some suspicion, some hint of the mischief Peter Bianco's enemies might be up to, made her head right to the gallery. Maeve had been plenty mad about him leaving.

Mike Payne waved as he came down the corridor. "I thought you might be here."

As she approached the open front of the gallery, Polly screamed.

"No!"

Two lanky boys in black jeans and jackets and one small person were busy threatening Mandy in the gallery, waving baseball bats and paint spray cans.

"Maeve," she whispered. She gulped. "Maeve," she shouted.

The small one in the middle of the fracas, wielding two cans of spray paint, turned and spotted Polly. She frowned, her eyes darting from the two boys wearing dragonfly earrings, holding their bodies like boxers on alert, and Polly.

"What do you want, kid? Peter's gone. Game over. Just making sure the stupid guy never forgets me." The vandals turned toward the paintings.

A small audience had gathered behind Polly. Mike stood by her shoulder.

"Why'd you do it, Maeve?" Polly asked.

"I don't know what you're talking about. I haven't done anything." She looked to the two boys for support. "Yet."

Mandy gripped the edge of the counter. Her earphones lay on the shiny surface. "You scared me."

"Why don't you just leave while you have the chance, while you have any sense left?" Mike Payne suggested. "Peter's gone – he's married – he never promised you anything, Maeve."

"Why'd you do those nasty things?" Polly asked again.

"I didn't start any of it," Maeve said. She looked to the two teens standing nervously behind her, baseball bats gripped in their hands. Even from the distance

Polly could smell the cigarette smoke, liquor, and unwashed body odour from them. One had terrible acne and the other boy needed a shave.

Polly shook in her boots. "You helped these guys though. Trash the mural. Smash those cars and the bus shelter, vandalize the office. I don't get it."

"You wouldn't, would you, kid?" Maeve laughed, but what she was saying wasn't funny. "You're too innocent for words, aren't you? The Innocent Polly McDoodle. Blinking artists think they're so smart. Even Bruce and Josh turned out to be wimps. Peter is all talk. I at least make wearable art. I'm the pro."

She turned and hollered, "Smash the family group. I hate that one." The Dragonflies hesitated, stared around them, and spotted the family picnic.

What could Polly do? Had Kyle found the police? Where was he?

"Don't start anything you can't finish," Mike leapt on the closest Dragonfly. Polly tried to grab the spray cans out of Maeve's hands as the girl pointed them at the offending canvas.

"The police are on their way," one bystander cried out.

Polly felt Maeve pull away from her and fall, felt a fine mist of black paint coating her old T-shirt. She ran to the hallway to hunt for help. Patrick Connelly and another uniformed officer stood framed in the double doors. Kyle stood behind them. Polly waved madly.

"Help!"

The Dragonfly with the bristly chin broke away from Mike. He dashed out of the gallery, saw the police, and turned to warn Maeve, who was picking herself up, and the other boy, the one with pimples, who seemed frozen to the floor over by the family painting. He moved suddenly, running out of the gallery.

The three vandals rammed Patrick and the other policeman, sent Kyle flying, and raced through the exit door. Kyle picked himself up off the floor as Polly ran up to him. "Are you all right?"

Kyle shook his head, pointed to Polly's spray painted T-shirt and laughed.

Patrick followed the three vandals out the door.

"They'll get away!" Polly screamed. "We have to go after them."

"I don't think they'll get far," said Kyle. "Look."

Polly stared through the window. Two cruisers and four police officers filled the space outside. Officer Connelly was busy putting Maeve into one of the police cruisers. The other two vandals were being placed in the back of the second car.

Polly and Kyle high-fived. The crowd gathered by the exit cheered and clapped. "I bet you'll get a reward," someone shouted.

Polly didn't think so. She and Kyle checked out the gallery. Mike was helping the owner straighten things up. Two of Peter's pictures were crooked. Some spray paint had splashed the white wall. The baseball bats lay on the grey carpet. Thanks to Mike and Polly, the vandals had not been able to destroy any of Peter's art.

"Good work," the gallery owner said. He was holding a shivering Mandy in his arms. "My daughter was sure frightened. She's had too much excitement, eh?"

"I'll stay and help here," Mike Payne said.

"Thanks, Mike," Polly said.

"Anytime, Polly."

Polly grinned and made her way with Kyle toward the mural. They had a lot to report. She wiped her hands together as if she had just tidied up a load of dishes. She was more like her mom than she thought. She liked an island of order in the middle of chaos.

She had one last thing to work out. But she needed her friends to help.

When she, Kyle and Erin reached the mural, Isabel was already being interviewed and photographed by the newspaper reporter. So the three of them sat around one of the tables at the edge of the Seniors' Centre.

"WHAT ABOUT THE TREE FORT?" Polly asked. "What will we do for the McDoodle, Clay, and Associates office?"

"We were getting pretty big for it," Erin allowed.

"I know, but I loved that old fort." Polly didn't go on, but to herself she thought that losing the fort was like losing a big chunk of her childhood, her innocence. Maybe there would never be an Innocent Polly McDoodle again. She sighed.

Kyle looked at her sympathetically. "Remember when I fell off the ladder and broke my ankle?"

"That was in Grade Two," Polly said.

"You left a tuna fish sandwich out there," Kyle laughed. "In Grade Four."

"The place stunk for a week," sighed Polly. "Life won't be the same without the fort."

Kyle just nodded. "What a time we've had."

"You can say that again," murmured Polly. She'd met the Biancos, who had become close friends for a while and now were gone. She had tried to help Chris, but had gotten into trouble because of it. Kyle would say that had been presumptuous, poking into someone else's life like that. She had learned not to judge people too quickly, even when their house was messy. She had figured out that some of her mother's rules about keeping clean and tidy were really all right.

She was changing. This summer she had put on a couple of pounds in interesting places and added a couple of inches to her height. In less than a month, she would be in Grade Seven.

"Maybe we could talk to the apartment co-op committee and see if we could build a bike shed with a tree fort, playroom, and patio on top." Kyle was drawing a plan in his notebook with a small ruler and a sharp pencil. "Suitable for bigger kids."

"Wouldn't it be too expensive?" asked Erin. "Where would we get the money?"

"Good question," mused Polly. "Interesting idea though, Kyle."

"Well, we're problem solvers, aren't we?" Kyle chewed sunflower seeds.

"We'd have to work with the grown-ups," Erin said. "It might be a challenge."

"No problem," said Polly. "After all we're pretty incredible...."

"Designers and planners." Kyle held up his preliminary drawing.

"And detectives," added the Not-So-Innocent Polly McDoodle.

acknowledgements

THIS IS A WORK OF PURE FICTION.
There is a real Kingsway Garden Mall in
Edmonton. However, I have taken great
liberties with the types of retail establish-
ments and placement of customer services. My Kingsway Mall is a composite
of both Westmount and Kingsway. I trust
no one will be offended. The historical
data about the Hudson's Bay Company
sale is true.

about the author

MARY WOODBURY is the bestselling author of two previous Polly McDoodle mysteries – *The Intrepid Polly McDoodle* and *The Invisible Polly McDoodle* – as well as *Jess and the Runaway Grandpa*, shortlisted for the Silver Birch Award in Ontario and named an Outstanding Title of the Year for 1997 by the Canadian Children's Book Centre. Her other titles include *A Gift For Johnny Know It All*, *Where in the World is Jenny Parker?*, and *Brad's Universe*. She has also published a short fiction collection and a book of poetry for adults.

about the cover artist

WARD SCHELL is an artist-in-residence at the Neil Balkwill Civic Arts Centre in Regina, where he teaches drawing, painting, and cartooning. His recent cover illustrations for Coteau include the juvenile fiction novels, *The Intrepid Polly McDoodle*, *The Half-Pipe Kidd*, *Thunder Ice*, *Willow Creek Summer*, and *Jess and the Runaway Grandpa*, and the David Carpenter novel *Banjo Lessons*.